"Miss Neville has caught the everyday life of children in a city environment and has told it well and with understanding."—*Childhood Education*

"Another refreshingly honest city story by the author of the Newbery Medal winning IT'S LIKE THIS CAT."
—*Commonweal*

"The shifting patterns of power plays within the gang are fascinating, as are the stratagems that the children use to maintain their privacy against adults."—*Saturday Review*

". . . a deftly sketched, knowledgeable evocation of the complicated, half-secret, half-public life that city children make for themselves."—Chicago *Tribune*

". . . a story noteworthy for its integrity, humor, and lively characterization."—Chicago *Sun-Times*

Other Books by

EMILY CHENEY NEVILLE

BERRIES GOODMAN

FOGARTY

IT'S LIKE THIS, CAT
Newbery Award Winner, 1964

TRAVELER FROM A SMALL KINGDOM

THE SEVENTEENTH-STREET GANG

THE SEVENTEENTH-STREET GANG

by
EMILY CHENEY NEVILLE

Pictures by
Emily McCully

A HARPER TROPHY BOOK

Harper & Row, Publishers
New York, Evanston, San Francisco, London

To G. T. N.

THE SEVENTEENTH-STREET GANG

Text copyright © 1966 by Emily Cheney Neville

Pictures copyright © 1966 by Emily Arnold McCully

First published in 1966. 5th printing, 1970.

First Harper Trophy Book printing, 1972.

Standard Book Number: 06–440019–0

Contents

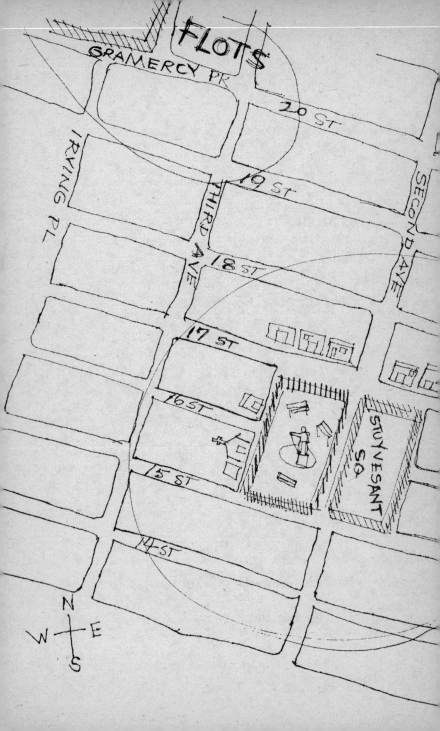

FOOT
BRIDGE

PIER

SEVENTEENTH ST GANG TERRITORY

FIRST AVE

1

The War with the Flots

Minnow squatted on the front steps, her bright crow's eye searching the block for anything bright and interesting, anything that moved. Below her Ivan played with his new model car and looked nervously over his shoulder, like a mouse, always ready to take cover.

Minnow checked the doorways of her friends' houses, stretching up Seventeenth Street toward Second Avenue. Nothing much moved. The house farthest from her own, near the corner of Second Avenue, was C.C.'s. His real name was Clement Charles Vanderpane, but he hoped no one knew. He was older than Minnow and sort of the boss of the Seventeenth Street bunch of kids, in a nice way.

Next to C.C.'s came Louise's house. Minnow was sure that Louise's family, the DeWitts, were the richest people on the block. They had a nurse *and* a maid, and their doorknob was always polished and the windows gleamed. But there was no action in front of Louise's house. She was stuck indoors with the mumps. Her best friend, Toby, in an apartment building a little closer, was probably on the phone talking to her.

Junior's house came next. It had a front stoop, like Minnow's own, but the steps were cracked and never swept. Bits of rubbish swirled on them in the wind. Junior came out the door. He looked toward Minnow, hunched one shoulder in greeting without taking his hands out of his pockets, and walked the other way, down to C.C.'s house.

Minnow hunched her own shoulders irritably. Everyone else had a best friend. Junior had C.C., Toby had Louise, but all *she* had was Ivan. She was actually quite fond of him, and she didn't mind playing with him almost every day.

2

It was really more like taking care of him, though, she told herself. He was two years younger than she, and besides he simply was a mouse. She watched him now. He was pushing a big nail along a crack in the sidewalk and crooning to himself: "B-r-rrm, b-r-rrm, b-r-rrm —PONG! B-r-rrm, b-r-rrm, b-r-rrm—PONG!"

On the third PONG, Minnow jumped like a frog from her step and lit with her right foot directly in front of Ivan's excavating nail.

His black eyes looked up at her, gentle and slightly worried.

"Get up! Someone's coming!" Minnow hissed at him.

"Why? What'll they do?"

"Nothing, silly. Look, you stand over here." Minnow led him to the edge of the curb by a lamppost. She tied one end of her skip rope to the post, about a foot off the ground, and told Ivan to stand there and guard it. She laid the rope on the sidewalk and held the other end of it herself, hiding in behind the stoop.

"I don't underst—" Ivan began.

Minnow explained. "We're toll collectors. We collect toll from everyone who walks along this block. You don't have to say anything. Not anything at all, see?''

Ivan nodded. He glanced up the block and saw an elderly couple walking toward them, obviously taking their afternoon stroll. They looked across at Stuyvesant Park, but it was a windy March day, and they apparently decided against walking in the park. They continued down the block toward the children. Just before they came to the rope, Minnow raised it to the level of their knees and said, "Stop here to pay toll, please.''

"Gracious, child!'' the old lady gasped. "You could have tripped us right up with that rope!''

Minnow said, "I know I *could* have, but today I'm not a tripper, I'm a toll collector.''

The lady sniffed irritably, but her husband looked as if he were hiding a grin. Very seriously he said, "You haven't told us how much the toll is. I don't know if we can afford it.''

"Oh, it's only two cents each. Really not much at all for a nice block like this.''

The lady exclaimed, "The idea! This is a public sidewalk! Get your rope out of our way now, little girl. Come along, Harry.'' She poked at his elbow.

4

He removed his elbow and stroked his chin. Minnow blew a wisp of hair out of her eyes. She looked up at the elderly man out of the tops of her eyes (it was what her mother called "batting her eyes at people"). She said, "I have to make money to help my friend. He can't talk."

"He can't talk at all?"

"Not a sound." Minnow shook her head sadly.

"And what do you do with the money?" the old man inquired, and Minnow had a suspicion he didn't believe her.

She smiled. "Oh, I buy him chewing gum so his jaw will get exercise. Otherwise he'd just stand like that the whole livelong day." She nodded at Ivan, who stood there with his sad eyes and his mouth buttoned up.

"Come along, Harry. This is nonsense!" The lady poked at him again.

He reached in his pocket and produced a nickel, which he handed Minnow. "There you are. It's a pleasure to contribute to a worthy cause."

"Thank you, sir. You can come back free—special round trip rate." Minnow went over to Ivan with the rope, and the couple walked along.

6

A few paces down the street, the old lady looked back at the children, who were chattering together. She exclaimed, "You see! I knew she was a shameless little liar! That boy can talk as well as anyone." The old man laughed and waved goodbye to them.

Ivan walked over to the stoop with the free end of the rope and said, "It's my turn to collect now. You be the one that can't talk."

Minnow was about to protest, but she looked down the block and saw C.C. and Junior coming. She didn't think they would pay toll anyway, so she said, "All right. It's C.C. and Junior. I'm going to hide in the bear's cave. Tell them if they don't pay the toll, I'll let the bear out."

Ivan wasn't at all happy about that bear, which he was sure lived in the dark cave place under his front stoop. He wanted to tell Minnow not to go in there, but she'd already gone. He looked up to watch C.C. and Junior.

C.C. was built like a half-size football star, broad shouldered and narrow hipped. He had sandy colored, bristly hair and walked with an easy, heads-up stride. Junior was about the same height, but much more slender, with dark hair

7

and black eyes. Unconsciously he sidestepped and danced along the sidewalk, avoiding the cracks.

When they reached him, Ivan raised the rope and quavered, "Halt and pay the toll!"

C.C. looked down at him and said, "Gonna make me?"

With both feet together, Junior jumped nimbly over the rope and jumped over it again backward. "I go for free!" he said.

"She—she said she'd let the bear out if you didn't pay," Ivan said. He looked at C.C. appealingly. He liked C.C. because C.C. didn't tease him about being a scaredy-cat.

C.C. shouted into the cave, "Hey, Minnow! Let's see that old bear! Bring him out."

Minnow came out. "He can't go outside today. I always give him a shampoo on Saturdays, and he'd catch cold."

"You're nuts," said C.C. "What're you doing anyway?"

"Collecting toll. Look." Minnow showed him the nickel and explained the system.

Junior was quite impressed. "Pretty neat. Let's collect some more."

They put up the rope again and took turns collecting, but they only got three more pennies. Minnow said, "People won't pay with you guys here. You're too big. I tell you what; let's go to the park. Ivan's mother won't let him go with just me, but she would with you two."

They got permission from Ivan's mother and started down the block.

"What're we going to do in the park? I haven't got a ball or anything," said C.C.

Minnow said, "We don't need a ball. We'll have a war with the flots." She said this as if it were an ordinary thing that anyone would know, not something she'd just made up.

"The *whats*?" said Junior.

"Whoever heard of flots?" said C.C.

"I did. Come on, you'll see." Minnow skipped into the lead, with Junior behind her, then C.C., and Ivan last. When she came to Junior's stoop, she climbed up the steps, slid over the railing, and came down the tiny bits of steps on the outside. The others did the same. They went up the next stoop too and came down and stamped on the coal hatch door beside it. It made a good clang. There were only five houses with stoops

9

left on the block. Most of the houses, like Louise's, had been remodeled so that they came down straight in front and left a good wide sidewalk. The few stoops that remained jutted into the sidewalk as fortresses or mountain ridges, with secret caves underneath.

C.C.'s stoop was a little different from the others, as it had a low, walled yard beside the steps. They all walked around the top of the wall, climbed the steps, and then banged down onto the coal hatch door on the other side.

Immediately the ground floor window was flung up, and a man stuck his head out. "You kids get outa here! You bang that door anymore today, I'm calling the cops!"

"We only did it once," said C.C.

"Don't get fresh!"

Minnow raised her arm from the elbow and pointed her index finger at the man. "Flot," she said. He slammed the window down.

The other children ran across the street to the park, and Minnow followed them unhurriedly. She cast her eye over the various mothers and nurses. "Lots of lady flots in here. They sit on the benches like fat puddings. You can be standing here, just minding your own business and eating your ice cream, and they say, 'Little girl, your face is dirty. You better go home and wash it.' "

Ivan said, "My mother sometimes brings a washcloth."

Minnow sniffed. "Huh. *I* tell them my face isn't washable, it comes out in spots."

"Do they chase you?" Ivan asked.

"Nah. Flots can't *do* anything. They just yak, yak, yak, and say they're going to call the park man or the cops."

"What if the park man gets me?" said Ivan.

"Then you'll be a hostage in the war, and we'll rescue you."

"I'm not sure I want to be in a war," said Ivan.

"Brace up, pal. I'll take care of you," said C.C.

They all climbed up on the statue of Peter Stuyvesant and hung out from it like gargoyles, to make faces at three little girls with doll carriages playing below. Pretty soon the park man came and told them to get off the statue. One of the girls with a carriage said, "See, I knew you weren't allowed. *I* never climb up there."

"You can't. You're just a baby," said Junior.

11

He put his thumbs in his ears and waggled his fingers at her.

"I'm not, I'm not a baby!" she wailed.

Her mother stood up and shouted at Junior. "You leave my little girl alone! Go on away from here!"

Junior backed off a little and went on making faces. Minnow walked up to the little girl and said, "Oh, you poor thing. Your mother is a flot, your dolls are flotties, and you're going to live in Flotsville forever."

The little girl stuck her lip out. "I do not. I live on Eighteenth Street."

"Oh, no, you're from Flotsville."

"I am not!"

The child's mother stood up again and came over, waving an umbrella. "You kids get away from here! Go on! I'll call the park man."

"Call him," said Minnow. "His telephone number is Flotsville 8-2000."

They ran off then, giggling and war-whooping, and went down to the end of the park where the bushes were thickest, and started making a fort.

After a while C.C. said, "No one's attacking us, and it's getting cold."

13

Ivan said, "I think we ought to go home. Maybe it's suppertime."

Minnow put her cap on the end of a stick for a banner and announced, "The flot-fighters march home victorious!"

They marched across to their own block and were about to separate to go to their houses, when they noticed a large transcontinental moving van backed in at the middle of the block. The men were easing out an enormous piece of furniture all wrapped in quilts.

"Hey, a grand piano!" said C.C.

"I bet it won't go through the door," said Junior.

He was right. With many shouts of "Okay, Mac!" "Watch it!" "Set her down!" the men plunked the great box on the sidewalk. One man went inside and soon appeared at a window. With a screwdriver and a hammer he took the whole window out and let down ropes. The other movers secured the ropes around the piano. The children pressed in close to watch.

A correct, formal-sounding voice said, "You children stand back. You might get hurt."

A man in a black overcoat with a velvet collar

was standing at the top of the stoop. Even Minnow looked at him with a certain amount of
respect. They all moved back.

A moving man turned around and roared,
"You heard the gentleman! Go on! Beat it! Get
lost! You could get hurt around here." He
nodded to the gentleman in the doorway and
added, "You gotta yell at these kids!"

The children moved a few steps further away
and Minnow said, "You don't own this sidewalk,
you flot you!"

The mover raised his arm. "Don't get wise
with me, kid! Beat it!"

A boy came out the front door and stood beside the gentleman. He was about C.C.'s age but
taller and thinner, and he was neatly combed and
had on a dark suit. The children didn't notice
him much, though, because they were looking at
his dog. It was a huge boxer with big white teeth
that protruded over his black upper lip. He was
straining at the leash to get down the steps to
the street. The boy could hardly hold him.

Ivan let out one yelp of panic and ran for
home. The boy scrambled down the steps with
the dog pulling him, and he shouted over his

15

shoulder to his father, "*We'll* keep the bystanders back, Dad!"

The great dog rushed toward the children. C.C. and Junior sprang up the outside of the next stoop and hung out from the railing. Minnow, who had had big dogs of her own, stood still. She was just beginning to have doubtful second thoughts—maybe all big dogs weren't friendly—when the man in the black overcoat shouted, "Hollis! Stop that! Come back here with Khan." The boy frowned at Minnow and regretfully hauled in the dog and turned around for home.

C.C., who always noticed other boys' names because he hated his own, caroled from his perch, "Oh, Hollis! Run along home, Hollis!"

Then he had a better idea. He started singing, "Deck the halls with boughs of Hollis . . ."

Minnow took it up: "Fa la la la la, la la la— *flot!*"

From the top of his stoop Hollis glowered at them once and went inside.

2
The Best Friends

The sun had set, C.C. and Junior had gone home, and Minnow realized that her knees and sneakered feet were really very cold. They had been for quite a while. She started for home, but looked up when she heard a rap on a window overhead.

Louise DeWitt was sitting at her window. Her nose pressed to the glass made a pinkish-blue blob. Aside from the blob nose effect, she was a pretty girl. She had beautiful hair, a dark reddish brown, which curved silkily around her face from a point in the middle of her forehead.

Her chin jutted out in a nice balancing point.

She opened the window and tried to shout in a whisper. "Who was that with the dog?"

"His name is Hollis. He's a flot," said Minnow.

"Wha-at?"

"He's—"

Minnow saw Miranda, the DeWitt's nurse, appear behind Louise. L uise shouted, "I can come out tomorrow," and then the window was pushed down. Miranda was really the nurse for Louise's little brother, but she still bossed Louise around.

Minnow shook her head and imitated the clucking grown-up's tone of voice. "Tch, tch, tch, that poor child. I don't know how she manages. Just rules, rules, rules all the time. Pretty soon she'll be a teen-ager and no more use at all." Minnow's teeth were actually beginning to chatter now, so she scuttled for home.

Inside the well-run DeWitt household, Miranda scolded: "If there is *one* thing your mother can*not* stand, Louise, it's shouting out the window!"

18

"There isn't *one* thing my mother can*not* stand, there are three million," Louise snapped back, which was unusual for her. "She can't stand noise, dirt, chewing gum, pizza, skate boards, blue jeans, or Toby, who happens to be my best friend, that's all! Mother goes to parties with *her* friends, but *my* best friend isn't even allowed in the house!"

"My, we are in a temper, aren't we?" said Miranda, but she just put it down to being indoors with mumps, and went out and closed the door.

Having let a few words fly, Louise felt better. She roamed around her room, looked out the window, and readjusted some of her china animals. Then she took the pillow off her bed, put it on the floor, and lay on it. Balancing on the back of her neck, she stretched her toes up to the ceiling and considered. "In the first place," she said to her right foot, "it's absolutely humiliating to have a nurse in the house at my age. She doesn't just take care of Jamie, she spies on me. Mother pays her to be a *spy,* that's what. She's supposed to find out every single wrong thing I do."

She swung her left foot forward and addressed it: "I do rather like Miranda, though. At least she's here when I come home from school, and Mom never is, and Miranda does iron my madras shirt more often than any of the others."

She switched her long legs back and forth like scissor blades. Mother is the one who really makes all the trouble, she decided. Miranda just thought she *had* to show her that diary Toby left here.

Toby always carried a diary, which was filled with proposed clubs, plots, and unflattering drawings and comments on certain grown-ups.

Louise pulled her knees down and hugged them and giggled. Toby's drawings were really good. They just weren't the kind your parents like, especially when one of them showed Mrs. DeWitt dressed in high heels, a fur hat, and a cigarette holder, taking a bath. This was the one Miranda had showed Mrs. DeWitt.

Toby Meyer just wasn't the kind of girl your parents like, come to think of it. She was sort of standoffish and superior, and her hair wisped out of her pigtails, and she looked at her own knees instead of at the grown-ups when she talked.

"*Look* at me, dear. You're talking to *me*." Louise mimicked her mother's voice.

She got up, put the pillow back on the bed, and went to her dresser. Despite all her grouching, a good many of her mother's ideas had rubbed off on Louise. She liked her room neat, with matching curtains and bedspread and a nice set of things on the dresser, and she liked to look nice herself. She put on her dark-green velveteen robe and brushed her hair till it shimmered in waterfalls on each side of her face.

"Maybe I look like Mona Lisa," she thought. Then she put the hairbrush down and erased the Mona Lisa from the mirror with a heavy frown. "Anyhow, I certainly ought to be allowed to ask my own best friend in, even if my mother doesn't like her. I'm not a baby anymore!"

She didn't waste any thought at all on the new boy next door.

After Hollis went inside, C.C. and Junior walked together back to C.C.'s house, where they spent some time putting together a do-it-yourself model radio. They did things together almost automatically, because they'd been friends since before they started school.

It had begun when C.C. was a little boy, playing with his trucks and soldiers out in the yard, with his mother sitting in the sun reading because she didn't like to leave him alone on the street yet. C.C. noticed a strange little boy standing outside the yard watching him, silent and beady-eyed.

"You want to play trucks?" C.C. asked after a while. The boy just stared. In fact he moved back a little, as if expecting them to chase him off. C.C. went on playing and divided his soldiers into a gray pile and a blue pile. He set up the blue army and then gathered the gray soldiers and brought them over to the boy.

"You be the gray army, okay?"

The boy glanced at C.C. and at his mother, still wary, but she smiled, and there was no doubt about what C.C. meant, so the boy climbed over the wall and started setting up the gray army. Soon they were both moving their men and knocking them down with shouts of POW! and BONG! and WHOP! Whatever C.C. said, Junior just grinned.

Then Junior realized C.C. was asking him a question. He repeated it several times, and he was getting impatient. Junior pushed the pile of gray soldiers quickly toward C.C. and started climbing back over the wall.

C.C.'s mother looked up from her book and said, in Spanish, "He wants to know how old you are."

Junior stared, goggle-eyed. Finally a stranger had said something he understood. For days he had been floundering around in a sea of meaningless sounds every time he left his own family. Mrs. Vanderpane's Spanish wasn't the same as his family's, but he could understand it. She told him she had been born in Italy.

After that Junior came to C.C.'s yard every chance he got, and pretty soon he came indoors to play too. C.C.'s mother was an actress and a singer. Sometimes she sang in Italian, sometimes in Spanish, and sometimes in English. Junior loved to listen to her and to watch her. He brought her bunches of dandelions from the park so she would have a bouquet of flowers to hold, like the singers he remembered in Puerto Rico. From both C.C. and his mother Junior gradually learned English. By the time he went to school, he could understand and speak it fairly well, but he wasn't ready to start reading it.

C.C. had started school full of enthusiasm. He liked the kids and the teacher, and he liked the blocks and paints and picture books. Then the teacher started concentrating on the black squiggles under the pictures, and after a few months she expected him to know some of them. School wasn't so good after that. C.C. guessed at words and usually guessed wrong, and other kids snickered. C.C. wasn't used to failure; he'd always been the leader. Pretty soon he stopped trying to guess words and just wouldn't answer.

The only kid who never laughed at him was Junior, who couldn't read at all. When the teacher asked him a word, he said, "It looks like a cockroach." The class all laughed, and the teacher didn't ask Junior any more words.

At the end of the third grade he and C.C. went into a special remedial reading class. Finally they had both learned to read, but they were behind in everything, and now they were repeating sixth grade. In the new strange class of younger kids they stuck together like glue.

24

Junior was the only one in the class who knew what the initials C.C. stood for, and C.C. was the only one who knew that Junior's real name was Angel Rivera.

After waving goodbye to Louise, Minnow ran down the block to her own house. She slapped her goose-pimpled knees as she ran to warm them up. She had on a snowsuit jacket, but early that afternoon when the sun was shining, she had decided to wear her camp shorts instead of her long pants. At her door she fumbled inside her jacket for the lanyard she wore around her neck. She'd woven it in day camp, and her door key was woven right into it so she couldn't lose it. She let herself into her apartment. Inside the door she stood quite still a moment and listened.

There was no sound. Minnow let out her breath in an angry puff and said to herself, You'd think a person's mother could get home by five o'clock at least.

However, she didn't waste any time moping. She was used to taking care of herself. She remembered her mother had a particularly cosy, furry wool skirt, a new one. She rooted through the closet, found the skirt, and put it on. It came almost to her feet, most comfortingly warm. She found a safety pin and fastened the skirt tight around her waist. Next she kicked off her sneakers and found a pair of her father's wool socks in his drawer. The sock heels bugged out in the middle of her calves, but she didn't notice that. She stuffed her feet into some boots and clumped out the door and down the steps. In the house next door, she rang Ivan's bell.

She had first rung Ivan's bell on a cold spring day two or three years before. She hadn't even known his last name, and the janitor had showed her the right bell, the one that said HEDGE. Ivan Hedge. How funny, she had thought. Because Ivan looked like a little animal who had just popped out from under a hedge.

Minnow had stepped into the hall and was looking up the stairs. Ivan peeped out from behind his mother. Minnow smiled at Mrs. Hedge and said, ''Will you mind me?''

''Mind—mind what?''

''Just mind me. My mother's gone to the dentist.''

''Oh, you mean take care of you. Goodness, are you all alone?''

Minnow looked behind her as if expecting a companion to appear. "Well, at the moment I am. Of course my cat is home asleep, and my mother left my sandwich in the icebox for lunch. She says I'm a big girl now."

Mrs. Hedge was horrified. She wouldn't have dreamed of leaving a child alone. She said, "All right. Would you like to come in and play with Ivan for a bit?"

"Yes, thank you," said Minnow, and she came up the stairs. "You don't have to mind me *much*. I mean, you can just say things like, 'Time to pick up your toys' or 'Time for lunch now,' and then I'll go home and get my sandwich. Okay?"

"Okay," said Mrs. Hedge, slightly bowled over.

Little by little after that, Minnow moved in, or at least came to play whenever her mother was out for long. It was true that she never made much trouble. In fact she kept Ivan busy and happy. Soon she persuaded Ivan to go outside to play with her on the sidewalk, and that was really a help. Mrs. Hedge had never wanted to send him out alone, and besides he was afraid of that bear under the stoop.

Mrs. Hedge had got to know Minnow's mother, and she liked her, although she disapproved of the free theories of child raising that prevailed in Minnow's house.

When Minnow clumped up the stairs with the red wool skirt trailing almost under her feet, Mrs. Hedge clapped her hand to her mouth. "Goodness! Isn't that the brand new skirt your mother just bought from that weaver down in Greenwich Village?"

"I guess so," said Minnow. "Pretty, isn't it? And *so* warm."

Over the years Mrs. Hedge had found that Minnow often came dressed outlandishly but that she was quite reasonable about changing. She said, "Look, dear, I have an old skirt that looks like a leopard skin that you can wear. I'll hang up your mother's new one before you tear it."

"All right," said Minnow amiably. She was warm now anyway. To Ivan she said, "Louise can come out again tomorrow. Us kids have all got to get organized and do something about that new boy with the big dog. We can't have him running us off the street. Besides, he's a flot.''

"I'm not having anything to do with the dog," said Ivan.

Minnow ignored him. She sat cross-legged on the floor and rocked back and forth dreamily. She chanted:

> *I'm making a plot*
> *To fix the flot.*
> *Oh, when I make a plot,*
> *He'll be on the spot.*
> *Wham!*

" 'Wham' doesn't rhyme," said Ivan. "Anyway I'm not going near the dog."

Minnow looked at him with exasperation. "Ivan, why *do* you have to be such a mouse?"

"Well, I can't help it. Anyway the boy might turn out to be nice. You can't tell, so why do we have to have a plot?"

"We just do. A plot for a flot." Minnow started humming again but was interrupted by the doorbell. Her mother had come to call her for supper.

—

3
Hollis Comes To Call

The next day, when Louise could finally go outside again, Miranda took care to remind her that
she wasn't allowed to go into Toby's house.
Louise didn't even answer. Toby was waiting
for her right outside the door, and Louise said,
"Let's move down the block aways, so Miranda
won't rap on the window and shake her finger at
me every five minutes."

"You really have a tough time," Toby said.
"Nobody else gets 'not allowed' to do so many
things. Someday she won't allow you to breathe."

"I know," said Louise. It was a distinction of
a sort.

"It seems like ages since I've been out," she continued. "What's been going on?"

"Nothing. Absolutely nothing. You can look in my diary and see. It's just been dead around here."

They sauntered down the block and found Ivan cleaning out another crack in the sidewalk with his nail and Minnow skipping rope.

Minnow said, "I made up a new skipping rhyme, all by myself. Listen:

> *Whick, whack, spit.*
> *Minnie had a fit,*
> *Because she couldn't knit.*
> *Knit one, purl one, knit two, purl two,*
> > *knit three—*

You go as far as you can."

Louise laughed. Toby said, "How boring."

Minnow suddenly shouted, "Hey, look! The flot's out!"

Louise and Toby thought she was just making up more nonsense, but they looked up the block.

There was Junior, hanging onto the outside

of one of the stoops. Opposite him C.C. was perched on the hood of a parked car. In the middle of the sidewalk stood Hollis and the big dog.

Hollis sneered at the two boys. "Not scared or anything, are you?" Then he walked across the street and into Stuyvesant Park.

C.C. and Junior saw the other kids and came down to join them.

"We've got to do something about that kid. He won't let us walk on our own sidewalk!" C.C. blustered.

Junior said, "That dog is a trained killer, I can tell. I've seen 'em on TV. They use them to catch escaped prisoners."

"If the dog really bites, you can call the police," said Toby.

C.C. and Junior looked irritated. "We don't need the police. We'll take care of that guy ourselves."

Minnow said, "It's perfectly simple. We'll just make him the first target in the war on the flots."

"Listen, goofy, this is serious. It's not one of your games," C.C. said.

33

"I'm perfectly serious. Every time one of us goes by him, we'll hum 'Deck the halls with boughs of Hollis,' the way we did yesterday. We'll drive him crazy. Pretty soon he won't dare come out."

"Hollis? Is that really his name?" Toby looked thoughtful and scribbled a few words in her diary. Then she said, "Let's leave a note on his door saying, 'Oh, Hollis. What a doll is Hollis.'"

They all cheered, and Toby wrote out the rhyme in large block letters, and they left the note on Hollis's door. Then they tried to think up some more rhymes, but Hollis was a hard word to find rhymes for.

Toby flipped to a new page in her notebook. "Making rhymes isn't going to be enough anyway. We might as well get organized for this campaign. We'll have meetings every Saturday morning to plan strategy for the weekend. C.C. can be the captain, I'll be the lieutenant, and—"

"I'll be the buzz bomb," interrupted Minnow. "I'm going over in the park to spy on them."

She ran across the street and Toby said, "Let her go. She isn't really any use in a club."

34

Late the next afternoon Louise was in her room studying when her mother came back from shopping. She had what looked like a shoe box in her hand, and Louise eyed it hopefully.

Her mother said, "Guess what? A girl I used to know at school just moved into an apartment next door to us. I bumped right into her on the street. She's married and her name is Rourke now, and they have a son your age named Hollis. Have you seen him outside? He has a big dog he walks."

"I haven't seen him," said Louise. She was always promising herself not to tell any more lies, but then someone asked her an unexpected question, and out one came. Well, she thought, Mother certainly wouldn't like it if I said, Yes, I've seen him and we're all planning a war on him.

"Louise! Stop daydreaming and pay attention, for goodness sake! I said, I asked them over for a drink or tea or something Wednesday afternoon."

"Uh—the boy—uh, Hollis, too?"

"Yes, of course, and don't 'uh.' I've told you a hundred times. Also, I remembered you didn't have any decent shoes, so I stopped in Saks.''

Louise jumped up and took the box. The only shoes she had that her mother called 'decent' were black patent leathers, which she hated and which were finally too small. If these were more patent leathers . . . she opened the box, and they weren't. They were red flats, with neat toes. Louise slipped one on and looked down her leg, and she glowed.

Mrs. DeWitt said, ''You remember and be pleasant to Hollis tomorrow. His mother wants him to go to dancing school too, so he'll probably go with you next Friday.''

''The boys all hate dancing school,'' Louise said.

''They'll soon be changing their minds about *that*,'' said Mrs. DeWitt as she went out the door. The I-know-better-than-you tone of voice annoyed Louise, but she remembered to thank her mother for the shoes.

So, what'll I talk to Hollis about, besides the war with the flots, she giggled to herself. Maybe he's interested in sports cars or records. Most boys are.

Louise was generally talkative and sociable, so

she didn't worry about it much. She put on both her shoes and admired them.

When the doorbell rang Wednesday afternoon, Louise answered it and brought the Rourkes into the living room. The two mothers exclaimed all over again about what a small world it was—imagine the two of them living right on the same block. Then they started talking about the good old days at Walden School, and the two fathers looked vaguely uncomfortable until they had their tea and could get off together and compare notes about their banking and law businesses.

Louise was about to ask Hollis where he went to school, but she remembered she had started several conversations like that at dancing school, and they hadn't come to much. So she said, "For my birthday I got the new Kermit and Karen record. It's their third. I didn't think it was nearly as good as the first two. They're really slipping, I think."

"I never liked them much anyway," said Hollis. "I think The Edge Singers are much better."

"Gee, do you? I bet maybe you're right."

Louise looked at him admiringly. "Everyone went so nutty about Kermit and Karen, but I bet it was just a fad. What other records do you like?"

Hollis quickly named several, some she had heard of and some she hadn't. He had taken piano lessons for years, and while he often groaned about practicing like any other kid, he really enjoyed music. He liked classical music the best, but he had learned to play a good many jazz and folk song pieces, and he had a big record collection.

Louise said, "I don't have an awful lot of records, but we could go play some." She felt sure he didn't particularly want to sit with the grown-ups and juggle a tea cup, and they'd both had a piece of cake, so there was really nothing more to stay for.

They went in her room, and while Hollis was sorting through her stack of records, Louise said, "Would you like a Coke? I figured maybe you'd had enough of that tea."

"Sure, thanks."

They each had a soda and listened to the records. Now that school was not just a nervous conversation opener, they got down to compar-

ing notes on their best friends, worst enemies, and toughest teachers.

After a bit Louise heard the grown-ups beginning to make polite departing noises. She asked Hollis, "Are you going to dancing school? Mom said something about it."

Hollis said doubtfully, "Well, is it any fun?"

"I like it," said Louise. "Lots of the boys hate it, because they won't try to learn how to dance."

"I like to dance all right. It's just the getting dressed up, and lots of new people. . . ." Hollis's voice trailed off.

"Why don't you come once? I can introduce you to some of the kids that are fun. You can always quit later if you don't like it."

"Well . . . all right. When is it, Friday?"

"Yes. I usually leave about six o'clock."

There was a short silence, and Louise crossed her fingers and hoped she wouldn't have to prod him to say he'd pick her up. Hollis looked nervous, but finally he said, "Well, we could go together. Shall I pick you up?"

Louise smiled wide. "Fine! I'll be ready at six."

4
Ivan's Bear

The campaign meeting on How To Get Hollis never met the next weekend. More than two feet of snow covered the street and park. It was the heaviest snowfall New York had had in years. It began on Thursday, and the next day none of the streets was plowed, no cars or taxis or buses ran, and the few people who went to work had to walk in the street. There was no school. Minnow and Ivan spent the day burrowing and tunneling outside their houses, frequently running indoors to get dry sets of mittens.

Saturday they decided to build a snow fort in

41

the park. Seventeenth Street still wasn't plowed out for traffic, so they could run back and forth across it all they wanted. There were plenty of children, and even willing fathers, to help make the fort. C.C. and Junior turned up, and then Toby and Louise. They took turns occupying the fort and attacking it, and then they all crowded inside—you could only get in through a tunnel in the back—and threw snowballs at people outside. Everybody in the park that day was dressed for snow, so no one minded.

"The flots don't come out in the snow," said Minnow. "They're home roosting on their radiators and clucking, 'Isn't it terrible!'"

From across the park they heard other children shouting, and Toby went out to spy. She reported back, "It's a lot of those tough kids from Sixteenth Street. I think they're coming this way! Come on, everyone, start making snowballs!"

They posted Ivan as a lookout, because he didn't look like a lookout. The others piled snowballs inside the fort. In a few minutes Ivan came scuttling back through the tunnel. "Here they come! Watch out!"

Minnow pressed her eye to the peephole in the front of the fort, and when the other gang of children were right in front, she gave the signal. C.C. and Junior and Toby and Louise stood up to throw.

They stood with their arms back and their jaws dropping: there were six kids in the other gang, all boys, and all rather big. C.C. and Louise just stood and felt foolish. Junior heaved his snowball at a man halfway across the park. But Toby let fly at the nearest kid in the other gang.

They all ducked, and Junior and C.C. glared at Toby and said, "You idiot! They'll murder us!"

Soon the fort was being bombarded by the Sixteenth Street kids. Minnow and Ivan crouched by the peepholes and squeaked, "Now!" whenever they saw an open target. The older four kept throwing and ducking, not scoring many hits.

"They've gone," Minnow announced suddenly. "We've won! Hur—"

She never finished the "hurrah," because the back wall of the fort crashed in under a human battering ram. The other members of the rival gang started throwing snowballs through the gap with yells of triumph. Ivan started crying. A snowball had hit him in the face.

"Let's get out of here!" yelled Junior.

C.C. grabbed Ivan by the hand. "Come on—to the bear cave!"

The cave that Ivan said the bear lived in, under his stoop, had been a frequent hideout for the children. Ivan had never gone in it himself, but this time he didn't even hesitate. C.C. just dragged him inside. The Sixteenth Street boys pelted them with snowballs and insults as they ran, but they couldn't hit them inside the cave.

After a bit Minnow crept out to look. "Whew! They've gone!"

Ivan sniffed, "They were bad flots. Let's not have any more war."

Minnow said, "*Those* weren't flots. My goodness, no!"

"They're just plain tough," said Junior. "And they're bigger than we are. We're not having any more war with *them*."

"Uh-*uh*!" C.C. agreed. "We leave them alone."

The coast was clear, and the four older ones

decided to go home. Minnow found a clean patch of snow and lay down in it to make angel wings. Ivan suddenly realized he was sitting all by himself, practically inside the bear's cave.

He jumped up, and then hesitated. He even took a step back into the cave and peered into the darkness. He went outside and said to Minnow, "The bear doesn't like it in that cave. He should have a nice snow house."

Minnow sat up on her angel. "I know—he can live in the snow fort. Then if those tough kids ever come back and try to use it, he'll eat them."

"Oh, yes!" Ivan clapped his hands. Then he said, "You take the bear over, okay?"

"Now, don't start worrying again, dear," said Minnow in her nursemaid voice. "You just run along and don't watch, and I'll bring him."

After Minnow said the bear was in the snow fort and had gone to sleep, Ivan came and helped her patch the broken back wall. Then he stood back and admired the fort, and a feeling of great satisfaction came over him, because the bear no longer lived under his front steps.

Then he felt something snuffling at his hand. It was an animal. He could feel its hot breath. In

one terrified bound he made the nearest park
bench and then looked back. It was Hollis's dog,
tugging on his leash, as usual.

Minnow came from around the snow fort, and
the dog strained toward her, its tongue hanging
out. Minnow stretched out her hand, palm up.
The dog sat down and raised its paw.

Minnow shook the paw. "How do you do, dog?
I'm Minnow. Isn't it nice to be out on a nice
snowy day when all the stupid people stay inside? How do you like living on Seventeenth
Street?"

While she talked to the dog, Minnow kept the
corner of her eye cocked at Hollis. He said, "He
likes it pretty well, but he misses having a yard
to run around in and other dogs to chase."

"You had a back yard of your own? You must
be rich."

"Um—no, where we lived was sort of in the
country. Almost everyone had yards."

"Did flowers pop up in the spring?" Minnow
had always lived in New York City, outside of
trips to the beach and summer camp.

Hollis said, "Sure. There'd be daffodils or
something out now."

"My!" exclaimed Minnow. The dog continued to offer his paw to be shaken, and Minnow asked, "What's his name?"

"Genghis Khan."

"*What?*"

"Genghis Khan—he was a Mongol general who fought all over Russia and Siberia back in the Middle Ages. He was really fierce."

"But *he* isn't fierce at all!" Minnow pointed to the dog.

"I know," said Hollis apologetically. "I thought he would be, that's all. I still think it's fun to pretend he's fierce. I watch all the people on the street scuttling out of my way. There are a lot of junky kids on this block, but I've got 'em scared."

Minnow saw that Hollis didn't recognize her as one of the children that had danced around him, singing and teasing. Her snowsuit and cap made a pretty good disguise.

"Do you live around here?" Hollis asked.

Suddenly Minnow couldn't decide whether she wanted to tell Hollis about herself and be his friend or whether she wanted to stick with the other kids in the plot to get him. It was sort of fun to have a plot going, and you could always get out of it later if it seemed to be a mistake. Uncertain, Minnow shrugged her shoulders and decided that, for the time being, she'd just make up a good story.

"I don't live around here," she said. "I'm just visiting for the weekend. I really live way up in New Hampshire. Up there we sometimes have snow higher than your head."

Minnow glanced around for Ivan, to poke him in case he was about to say she lived next door to him. He wasn't listening to her at all. He had his eyes fixed on Genghis Khan, and he had got off the bench and was sidling up toward the dog.

He stopped about two feet from where the dog was sitting placidly in the snow. Ivan said, "Doesn't his bottom get cold?"

"He doesn't seem to mind," said Hollis. Khan put his paw up towards Ivan, and Ivan got his courage up and shook it. A broad grin broke over his face.

"I'm not afraid, am I?" he said proudly.

"Of course not," said Hollis. "Well, I guess I better run Khan around some more. He needs exercise. It's too bad you don't live around here.

The kids seem to be a pretty crumby bunch in this neighborhood.''

Before Ivan could open his mouth, Minnow said, ''Maybe my family will move down here. They get terribly cold up in New Hampshire. Maybe I'll see you tomorrow anyway. So long.''

''What does he mean you don't live here?'' Ivan asked, after Hollis had walked away. Without waiting for an answer, he went on, ''See, I told you that boy might be all right, and now I'm not even afraid of the dog. Let's go find the kids and tell them we don't have to have a plot to get Hollis.''

''Um—well . . .'' Minnow stood frowning and trying to think. ''You know that bossy Toby. She'll say we're just babies, we don't know what we're doing. Or else she'll say we were traitors to go talking to Hollis at all. We better not say anything.''

''I want to tell them I'm not afraid of the dog,'' Ivan objected.

The really nicest thing, Minnow decided, would be to keep Hollis all for myself. He could be my very own friend, and no one else would know. Except Ivan, and he doesn't really count.

In the bright, enthusiastic tone that she knew always convinced Ivan, Minnow said, "I tell you what—let's keep it a secret! We won't tell them we've patted the dog or talked to Hollis or anything. Then when old Toby finds out she's done all that organizing for nothing, we'll just laugh and laugh."

"I want to show C.C. I can pat the dog," Ivan persisted.

"But don't you see? It'll be so much better. Someday when they're all running away from Khan, you can just saunter up to him and say, 'I'm not afraid.' " Seeing that Ivan still looked doubtful, Minnow hurried on, "Anyway, we can go tell the others about the bear. They don't know he doesn't live in the cave anymore. We've got to tell them he's in the snow fort now."

"Okay," Ivan agreed.

The afternoon had warmed up, and the snow was melting everywhere. They started toward home, and Minnow said, "Soon it'll really be spring. In the country flowers come up in the spring, but in the city new people pop up."

"Really?"

"Really."

At the park gate Ivan looked back at the snow fort and waved goodbye to the bear. Then a disturbing thought came to him. "When the snow all melts in the spring, what will happen to my bear?"

"He'll migrate. They go to the North Pole in spring."

"Good," said Ivan. "Come on, let's tell everyone I'm not afraid of the bear now."

5

Warpath to Gramercy Park

After he left Minnow and Ivan, Hollis walked twice around the park, kicking irritably at the snow. He wished they had never left their old home outside Philadelphia. He'd had a couple of best friends there that he could always do things with—skating and bicycling, and swimming in summer. In New York none of the kids seemed to want to do anything he wanted, and besides none of the kids in his school lived nearby.

He crossed the street and went past Junior, who was squatting in the snow modeling a snow statue of a dog. Junior tossed a snowball toward

Hollis and Khan, pretending he wasn't really aiming at them. Khan caught it in his mouth.

"Hey!" Junior looked surprised and admiring in spite of himself. "He can really catch!"

"I wouldn't try throwing another. I might not be able to hold him," Hollis said. He gave Khan a sharp tug and walked on. He felt uncomfortably aware of Junior behind him. Maybe the kid was just trying to be friendly, he thought; but then again, maybe he wasn't. Maybe right now he was getting ready to drill Hollis in the back of the neck with a hard snowball.

Actually Junior just muttered, "Snobby flot," under his breath and went on with his statue.

In the house, Hollis's father was reading the newspaper. Even though it was Saturday, he had on good gray flannel trousers and a clean shirt, and he looked trim and ready for anything. It was one of his convictions that people should always be alert and ready for anything. He was a successful banker, a good golfer and chess player, and he prided himself on his ability to handle other people.

The only person he felt that he didn't manage well was his own son. He could never understand why Hollis seemed to hold back and act afraid of so many things and people. Mr. Rourke looked at him now, the way he entered the room with his head down and his shoulders hunched. He frowned. No boy could *feel* confident when he went around *looking* like that.

"Getting to know some boys in the neighborhood, Hollis?" Mr. Rourke asked.

"Um—well, I was just talking to a couple of kids about Khan."

"Good. Khan'll help you make friends. Almost all kids like a dog. You could let him off the leash once in a while and show the kids how he fetches and rolls over."

Hollis grunted and said nothing, thinking how impossible it was to explain to his father that he used Khan to scare the kids off. Impossible to explain, in the first place, why he had to scare off any strange bunch of kids.

Mr. Rourke had some suspicions, though in the wrong direction. "There aren't any gangs of toughs bothering you, are there? I've seen one or two kids around I don't like the looks of. It's sort of a mixed neighborhood here."

"They're not particularly tough," said Hollis.

Mr. Rourke went on, "It's harder to make friends in a new neighborhood in winter, I think. Pretty soon it'll be spring, and all the boys will be out playing ball, and you'll get to know them."

"I'm not much of a ball player," said Hollis.

Mr. Rourke knew that, but it annoyed him even more for Hollis just to admit it. He tried not to let his voice get edgy. He had that familiar feeling that every word he spoke was just a drop of water spattering off a stone. Nothing sank in when he talked to Hollis. Still, he went on trying, pouring out the words: "Well, don't just give up! Try! You're well coordinated. Any boy who can dive as well as you can ought to be able to do well in other sports too. As soon as the weather warms up, I'll get out and catch with you."

Hollis had an immediate picture of his father standing out on the block playing catch with him, with all the kids watching. He could just hear his father, shouting hearty encouragement, and see himself muffing an easy catch.

"I guess I'll go do my homework," Hollis said, knowing his father couldn't object to that.

"Of course, I'm delighted you're doing so

well in school. The change in schools didn't
bother you at all," said Mr. Rourke. "But don't
forget that all work and no play . . ."

Hollis had already started down the hall. He
went to his room and buried himself in a book he
was reading for extra credit in history. It was
about a boy who was a bull dancer in ancient
Crete, back about 2000 B.C. The boy leaped onto
the bull's head and stood on his hands, gripping
the bull's horns, while all the people in the am-
phitheater cheered. Hollis read for a couple of
hours till he finished the book. Then his eyes felt
prickly and his head ached, and he felt vaguely
dissatisfied. No use wanting to be a bull dancer,
he thought. That was all four thousand years
ago.

He sprawled on his bed with his eyes closed,
picturing the boy poised over the bull. Then he
sat up and shook himself. It would really be
something like a diver poised on the end of a diving board, standing on his hands ready for a flip.
Hollis loved the moment of silence just before a
dive, then the clean, cold water, and the audience
clapping when you came up. Nothing like football or basketball, all bumping and shouting and
commotion.

There had been no Friday dancing class during the snowstorm, and now Hollis had most of a week to wait till the next one. He hadn't seen Louise again, and he began to feel more and more uneasy about the whole thing. He wished he'd never agreed to go. He tried telling his mother he wouldn't go.

"Nonsense, dear," she said. "At least give it a try. Besides, you promised that nice DeWitt girl."

There were several days of warm, steady rain, and the great snow all melted away. By Friday the air smelled of spring, and there were little red cattails on some of the trees in the park. Hollis came out of his door and sniffed the breeze and wished he could just go for a walk. Dutifully, however, he went to Louise's front door and rang the bell.

There was a short pause, and then he heard her clattering down the stairs inside. She came out smiling, and almost immediately pointed one foot in its new red slipper and said, "Look! New shoes! Isn't it wonderful—having spring and new shoes both?" She twirled around, breathing in the soft air, and her hair rippled about her shoulders as she twirled.

58

She knew she looked nice, and she felt good. Watching her, Hollis began to feel good too. He couldn't help it. They strolled along to the corner, swinging their arms and feeling as if they owned the city. Hollis said slowly, "You know, you'd think you would notice spring more in the country because of the buds and grass and birds and everything. But really it's more exciting in the city."

Louise thought, He doesn't just talk to make conversation, he has something to say. Aloud she said, "I never thought of that, but maybe you're right. I never spent spring in the country anyway."

"Really?" It was hard for Hollis to imagine someone growing up his whole life in the city. "I suppose you can get to like the city. But there are more things to do in the country. Like on weekends—we used to go on long bike rides in the spring. I can't find much to do around here weekends. What do you do?"

Louise said, "I usually do something with Toby. We ride bikes or roller skate."

"Who's Toby?" Hollis wondered if it was one of those two boys that always made fun of him. A taxi came and they got in.

Louise said, "Toby's my best friend. Only my mother doesn't like her, so we can't go in each other's houses, and she doesn't go to my school. Outdoors on Saturday is about the only time I can see her."

"Oh." Hollis could see he couldn't tag along with Louise and her best friend, and he couldn't think of anything else to say.

The taxi went along uptown, and they could see Central Park down at the ends of the blocks. That gave Louise an idea. She was sort of sick of hanging around the block every weekend. It would be fun to do something different with Hollis.

She said, "Maybe my mother would let me go bicycling in Central Park with you. There's a good bike track, but my mother's never let me go with any of the girls. She thinks we'd get knocked over the head or something."

"How about riding through all the traffic to get up there? Wouldn't she object to that?"

"Well, probably." Louise frowned. "We could rent bikes up there and take a bus up some Sunday."

"Okay. This Sunday?"

"All right. I'll ask my mother and call you."

They rode along, and Louise thought her mother would almost certainly let her go. Her mother was always sort of prodding her to do something with a boy, and especially *not* with Toby.

I'll have to think of something to tell Toby, she thought. I'll have to say it was Mother's idea and I couldn't get out of it. She briefly wished life didn't require so much planning and telling people so many different things.

Saturday was bright and sunny. Minnow knelt on the sidewalk near Hollis's house, drawing pictures with chalk. She hoped Hollis would come out now, while the other kids were not around, so she could talk to him some more. He wouldn't recognize her as the snow-suited little girl from New Hampshire (of course that little girl had gone on back to New Hampshire), because she looked entirely different now. She had on shorts and an old shirt of her father's which hung to her knees. It was belted in with a gold kid belt that her mother would be hunting high and low for pretty soon.

She decided she would tell Hollis she was the daughter of a penniless Greenwich Village actor. She could do some scenes for him from the play her father was rehearsing, especially a deathbed scene.

The only trouble was Hollis didn't come out. Instead Minnow saw Ivan coming up the block toward her, and Louise and Toby came out and sauntered over to the park. Minnow and Ivan continued chalking pictures on the sidewalk, until C.C. and Junior came along.

"The flot's father will bawl you out for chalking on his sidewalk," said C.C. "Anyway, let's go over to the park and see what's doing."

They joined the girls, and Minnow said, "Have any new children popped up? It's spring, you know. We ought to look for them."

"You're nuts," Toby grunted. Just then they heard shouts and catcalls from across the park. It sounded like the big boys from Sixteenth Street.

"We better migrate," said Ivan. "We don't want another war."

"You got a point there, pal," said C.C. The children slid off the rail and sauntered out of the park, trying to make it obvious that they had not been routed. As a matter of fact, the Sixteenth Street boys never even noticed them. They were busy arguing about stickball teams.

Back on their own block Toby said, "I know what! Let's go over to Gramercy Park and tease all those sissy kids that are locked in there."

Years before, Toby had walked past Gramercy Park, and a child inside had made a point of telling her, "This is a private park. You can't come in, because you haven't got a key." Toby had had it in for Gramercy Park kids ever since.

Ivan said, "That's a long way. I'll have to ask my mother."

"Me too," said Louise. She went and told Miranda they were going to Gramercy Park to see the daffodils in bloom, and C.C. walked down with Ivan to ask his mother. He assured Mrs. Hedge, Ivan's mother, that he'd watch out for Ivan crossing the avenues. They trooped along to Gramercy, stopping to swing around street signs and climb into the saddles of two parked motorcycles and mark their initials on dirty cars. Across Twenty-first Street from Gramercy Park, they paused in a little knot to make a plan.

A doorman immediately came out of the next building. "Can't play ball here, kids," he said. "Run along."

"We don't even have a ball!" said C.C., showing his hands.

"Beat it, you kids, I said. You don't live around here."

Deliberately, the children sauntered across the street. Last in line, Minnow turned around and crossed her fingers at the doorman the way she had seen a gypsy do. She said, "Flot. I hope you get warts."

Alongside the park they lined up, holding the bars and peering through. As soon as a couple of girls her age came by, Toby shouted to them, "Too bad you have to be locked up!"

"Is it something contagious, or are you all looney?" Louise yelled.

The two girls inside whispered together and ran off.

Minnow turned her attention to a little girl and boy digging in the dirt with their shovels and pails. She said, "My, my, that's too bad! You're just going to be covered with warts."

"What's warts?"

"All those dark spots on your hands. They grow."

The little boy said, "I don't care," but the little girl rubbed at her dirty hands and then ran off shouting, "Mommie, Mommie, fix my hands. They're warting!"

Toby looked up the street to the main park gate and saw the two big girls and several of their friends coming out. The Gramercy Park children pointed and shouted, "There they are! Let's get them!"

"Couldn't catch a butterfly!" Toby sing-songed, and the Seventeenth Street gang took off.

C.C. grabbed Ivan's hand and tugged him along. As they rounded the first corner of the park, C.C. glanced back at their pursuers. When he turned around again, he practically ran straight into Hollis Rourke walking Khan. Hollis, as usual, was walking with his head down and didn't see them till Ivan bumped into Khan.

There was a general muddle of boys and dog. Then C.C. jumped up, grabbed Ivan, and pulled him over to the curb. Minnow followed them. On the other side of the sidewalk, Junior and Toby and Louise jumped up on the stone step of the park railings.

Hollis found the aisle clear between the two rows of children. He caught Louise's eye, and that embarrassed him even more. He cleared his throat, twitched at Khan's leash, and marched on. He immediately ran into the pursuing group of children, and they swirled all around him. Then the two bunches disappeared around the next corner, whooping and jeering at each other.

Hollis trudged on alone, listening to the whoops of the children until they were swallowed up by the traffic noises of the city. He decided he wouldn't go bicycle riding with Louise. She probably thought he was a dope and only went to dancing school with him because she had to.

That evening, with a suspicious smirk around her mouth, Hollis's mother called him to the telephone. He said, "Hello" in his deepest word-swallowing mumble.

"Oh, hi!" Louise chirped. "I would have yelled to you this afternoon, but those silly kids were making such a noise. I asked my mother about bicycling tomorrow. She said okay. What time shall we go?"

"Uh—anytime you say."

"Well, I have to go to church, and then we have lunch. I'll meet you outside about two-thirty."

"All right." Hollis tried to think of something more to say, but finally finished with, "Uh—see you then. G'bye."

6
The Egg Approach

Junior was standing in C.C.'s yard, bouncing a ball and waiting for C.C. to come out. Hollis and Mrs. DeWitt, who had happened to come out of their houses at the same time, walked down the block and past Junior. Mrs. DeWitt glanced at Junior without changing her expression and said something to Hollis as she walked on.

Junior glared after them. She looks at me like I'm not there, he thought. Snobby flots, both of them.

C.C. came out, and Junior sounded off to him.

"I thought we were all going to get that kid anyway. What happened?"

C.C. shrugged. "Nothing, I guess. It snowed and we forgot."

They saw the rest of the kids gathered at the other end of the block and went down to join them. Junior said, "About that kid with the dog —what're we going to do?"

"Did that big fierce dog chase you again?" Minnow asked, winking at Ivan.

"Umm—no. I just don't like the looks of that kid," Junior said.

"Before we can do anything," said Toby, taking charge as usual, "we have to find out some things about Hollis. You know—what he's scared of and what he likes. Stuff like that. Does anyone know anything about him?"

"I do," said Louise. "He hates games with teams. He hates eggs, any kind, even hard-boiled. He plays the piano, and he won prizes for swimming and diving at camp."

The children gaped. "How do *you* know?" C.C. asked.

"I had to see him last Sunday, and he goes to

dancing school with me every Friday.'' Actually, Louise had had a very good time bike riding on Sunday, and that was when she had found out all the things Hollis liked and didn't like.

''Ugh! The things your mother makes you do!'' said Toby. ''Dancing school must be the bottom.''

''Well, it wasn't too bad. Of course I get sick of it, but actually he dances pretty well.''

''That proves it. He must be a flot,'' said C.C.

Toby said, ''If I were a boy, I'd *hate* dancing school.''

''I wouldn't, I'd love it,'' Minnow said. ''If I was dancing with a girl I didn't like, I'd stamp on her feet.''

''Come *on*,'' said C.C. ''This isn't getting anywhere. We've got to think of something to do about Hollis.''

Junior said, ''He doesn't like eggs. Let's throw eggs at him.''

''Yah!'' shouted the surrounding bunch of kids.

''We'll get in trouble if we really throw eggs,'' said Louise.

''Let's just break eggs on his front steps, and

when he comes out and steps in them, he'll get sick." That was Minnow's idea. She just couldn't resist adding to the plot.

Toby went into her apartment to get eggs, and they drew lots to see who would break them. Minnow and Junior won. The others scattered and found hiding places where they could watch Hollis's front door.

Minnow marched up the steps to the top. She cracked her egg on the doorknob and held it out at arm's length. SPLAT! It dropped and broke. Minnow ran down the steps and began doing a triumphant Indian war dance.

Junior opened his egg carefully onto the bottom step. Then he stood up and placed his heel in the middle of the yoke. Just then the front door opened. Mr. Rourke came out.

He stepped right into the egg Minnow had broken and slipped a little. He grabbed the rail to steady himself and looked down just as Junior was smearing his egg on the bottom step.

"You young hoodlum, you! Wait'll I—" He tried to wipe the egg off his foot and run down the steps after Junior at the same time. Junior took off. He started running down the street toward his own building, then crossed the street and disappeared around the corner.

Minnow had stopped her war dance to watch Junior. When she saw Mr. Rourke looking at her, she smiled at him. "My, he's a bad boy, isn't he?"

"I'll get the police on him! I thought this was a decent neighborhood!"

"I think it's quite decent, really," said Minnow. "Do you want to watch my Indian dance? I'm practicing for the pageant at school."

Mr. Rourke only grunted and stamped back into his house and slammed the door. Minnow went on circling and whooping.

The other children started popping out of their hiding places, and C.C. called to Minnow. "Stay hidden, everyone," she directed. "Maybe he'll send Hollis out to clean it up."

They all watched, but a maid came out with paper towels and a mop to clean up. She bent over, puffing and grunting, then straightened up and glared up and down the block. Faint shushes and snickers came to her, but she couldn't see any children.

The maid went in, and the children drifted

down the block toward the corner, where Junior was whistling to them.

"Weren't you scared when the man came out?" Ivan asked Minnow.

"He didn't know me. He just thought I was an Indian."

"He'll know *me* all right, though," said Junior. "I'm the only Puerto Rican kid on the block. If he goes to my father, Dad'll murder me. He's always preaching about not getting into trouble."

They all thought. Finally Toby said, "There are a lot of Spanish kids on Sixteenth Street. Let's all say it was one of them."

"How are we going to say it?" Junior objected. "If Mr. Rourke comes around to my apartment, he'll recognize me all right."

"That's easy. I'll go tell him right now," said Minnow. She skipped gaily back to the Rourke house. She hoped Hollis had come back and that he might open the door, though she hadn't decided what she would say to him.

The maid answered the door, and before Minnow could say anything, she snapped, "I don't want any more trouble with you kids!"

"*I* never make trouble, not me. I just want to tell Mr. Rourke who that bad boy was so he can send the police after him."

The maid looked suspicious, but she went to get Mr. Rourke. When he came, Minnow said, "I found out where that bad boy lives. He lives on Sixteenth Street. There are a lot of bad children over on Sixteenth Street. It's a *very* bad block."

Mr. Rourke cleared his throat irritably. "I suppose I'll have to get his name and go and identify him."

"Hmmm." Minnow looked as if she were trying hard to remember. "Chico—that's what I heard the kids call him. Chico—let's see—Chico Santa. Like Santa Claus—that's it."

"Oh." Mr. Rourke looked doubtful. "Well, thank you."

He started to close the door, and Minnow piped up quickly, "Why don't you send your son and his dog around to beat that boy up?"

Mr. Rourke frowned again. He began to suspect this snippety child was making fun of him somehow. He said, "No, that wouldn't do. Run along, now." He shut the door firmly behind him.

Minnow went back to report to the children. She said, "Junior's safe. I've got him all convinced to send the police to raid Sixteenth Street."

"Aw, Mr. Rourke'd never bother Junior anyway," said Toby. "But the main thing is *we* still haven't done anything about *Hollis*."

They all had to agree that that was true.

7
Minnow's Plot

Early in May the weather suddenly turned midsummer hot. One Saturday Minnow and Ivan set up a lemonade stand on the corner of Seventeenth Street and First Avenue. They didn't sell real lemonade, because they'd found that didn't pay. They used a five-cent envelope of artificial flavor and two cups of sugar which Ivan's mother gave them. She made them buy paper cups so they would be selling sanitary drinks, but they used the cups over and over until they looked really smudgy.

They had taken in eighty-five cents at five

cents a cup, and would have made more, except that bigger kids on the block kept raiding the stand. They knocked cups off the stand, tried to grab full cups, and one boy threw stones in the pitcher. Minnow fished them out and hurled them after him.

"We should call the police," said Ivan.

"Can't. We haven't got a license."

"You don't need a license to call the police."

"No, but you're supposed to have a license to sell lemonade." Minnow looked down at Ivan severely. "This is illegal lemonade. We're lemonade bootleggers."

"How come?"

"You can't go out on the street in New York City and sell one teeny little straight pin without getting a license and paying income tax. My father told me, and he's a lawyer." Minnow concluded her lecture and looked up, right into the face of Hollis Rourke.

He didn't seem to recognize her or Ivan. He said, "Boy, it's hot! Can I buy a drink?"

Khan flopped down on the sidewalk and pinned down a spilled paper cup with his paw so he could lick the sticky sweetness out of it. Minnow filled a cup for Hollis, and Ivan picked up the dirty cup and poured some more in it for Khan.

"That's five cents," said Minnow.

"Each?" asked Hollis.

"No, the dog's free. He's using a dirty cup."

"Besides, I like him. I'm not afraid, am I?" Ivan looked right at Hollis, and his pleased, pleading look was unmistakable.

Hollis said, "Say, aren't you the two kids I saw out in the park that day of the blizzard?"

"Sure we are!" said Ivan.

"But you said you were going back to live in New Hampshire, or someplace," Hollis said to Minnow.

Minnow thought fast. She could never bear to tell stories that were drab and ordinary, so she said sorrowfully, "I have to live here with friends now, until my mother gets well."

"Is she very sick?"

"Oh, yes. She's been in the hospital for weeks." Minnow let a little sob come into her voice. "I don't know if she'll get well. Maybe I'll have to live with Ivan here for always."

Hollis happened to look at Ivan. His mouth hung open and he looked completely bewildered.

Then Hollis saw Minnow kick him in the ankle.

Hollis began to get the pitch, but he kept his face very serious as he asked, "Did she have an operation?"

"Oh, yes, she's had several operations. Six doctors have operated on her."

"Including Dr. Kildare?" Hollis grinned.

Minnow's head jerked up, and she found herself blushing furiously as she saw him standing there grinning. "Go ahead and laugh, you big booby! I suppose you'd laugh if she was dying!"

"But she's not, is she?" Hollis said. "Come on, she lives right here with you, doesn't she?"

"It's none of your business what my mother does! Just drink your lemonade and go along!" Minnow snapped.

But Hollis had no place he wanted to go. "I'll have another glass of lemonade, please," he said and put down another nickel. Minnow tossed it in the change bowl with an angry clink, and Ivan poured the drink.

"It's so hot," Hollis went on. "Isn't there some place to go swimming around here?"

Ivan said, "I hate swimming in the pool. Boys duck me."

"You wouldn't be scared if you really learned how to swim well," said Hollis. "I could teach you if there was a pool."

"The pool's not open yet. Why don't you go jump in the river?" Minnow cackled. "Come on, Ivan. I'm sick of selling lemonade. You take the cups and the box, and I'll carry the pitcher and the money."

"We have to divide the money."

"I *know*!"

Hollis said, "So long. I'll see you again, now that I know you live here."

Minnow scowled, but Ivan said, "Okay, I'll see you again." He wished Minnow weren't dragging him home. He would rather have stayed with Hollis.

"If you think of a place to go swimming, let me know," Hollis called as they left him. He and Khan went on up the avenue.

Minnow and Ivan found the other four children sitting in the cool shade of Ivan's old bear cave. Toby said, "Did you pass the flot? He went past here, after letting that dog almost chew my leg off. We just got to the cave in time."

Junior said, "If we're ever going to get him,

we have to do it sometime when the dog isn't with him."

"Yeah," said C.C. "But the dog always *is* with him."

Louise didn't say anything. What she really wished was that Hollis would stop pretending the dog was fierce, and then they could all be friends, and she wouldn't have to keep pretending to Toby that she hated Hollis. It was getting tiresome.

Minnow wasn't tired of hating Hollis at all, though. She was just starting. She could stand almost anything better than being laughed at. She stood stock still with her finger to her forehead and thought hard.

"I know! It's easy! I'll tell him I know a place to go swimming, and of course no dogs are allowed."

"He wouldn't go anywhere with *you*," Toby said.

"He would too! Wouldn't he, Ivan? We were just around on First Avenue selling lemonade, and he bought a cup, and he asked us if we knew any place to go swimming, so there! Didn't he, Ivan?"

82

Ivan nodded obediently.

C.C. said, "Well, all right, but where do you know to go swimming? The pools don't open till June."

Minnow hadn't thought of that yet, but it came to her right off. "The river! The East River, of course!"

Ivan was goggle-eyed. "You can't tell him to swim in the river. It's too deep. He'll drown."

"Silly, deep doesn't matter if you know how to swim," said Toby.

"He's a champion swimmer anyway," said Louise.

"I'll bring a rope, just in case," said Junior.

"I'm not coming," said Ivan, and for once he really meant it.

Minnow was hopping with impatience. "Oh, stop jabbering! It doesn't matter if anyone swims or not, really. I'll just *say* that, so I can get him over to the East River without the dog. You can all be in hiding places over there and jump out at him! That'll show him!"

They jumped up, all pleased with the plot except Louise and Ivan. Louise decided when it was time to jump out at Hollis, she'd just stay hidden. Ivan said, "I think it's mean. I'm glad I'm not going."

"You're just scared to go near the river," said Minnow.

Just then Miranda came part way down the block and called to Louise, "Lunch time! Come along."

"Aw, gee. . . ." Louise acted very disappointed.

"Never mind," said Toby, quickly moving in to organize the plot. "We'll meet here right after lunch. We'll all stay hidden while Minnow asks Hollis. If everything's okay and he's coming, she'll give us a signal, and we'll all run over to the pier at Twenty-third Street. We'll hide just the other side of the footbridge over the East River Drive. Okay?"

"Lou-*ise*!" Miranda called again.

"Coming!"

"This'll be the signal," said Minnow. She plucked her crooked bangs straight up till the hair stood on end, then let go and twiddled her fingers.

"You always have to be so silly!" growled Toby.

Hollis, from his window, watched C.C. and Junior and Toby walk home. He wished that he either knew them or that they lived on some other block.

After lunch, when the other children had hidden, Minnow pranced up the steps to ring Hollis's bell. She felt very important, the center of the plot, the one who makes things happen.

Hollis answered the door himself. "Oh, you," he said.

"I think that's a very rude way to speak," said Minnow. "Don't your family teach you any manners?"

There was something pretty funny about being glared at by a little girl who hardly came to your shoulder, and Hollis grinned. He said, "Excuse me. Of course I would have said, 'Come in, Miss Butterflywing,' but I didn't know if your name happened to be Miss Butterflywing."

"It doesn't happen to be. It happens to be Min—uh, Minerva."

"That's a nice name. I'm glad you're not angry anymore."

"Oh, that was just a ten-minute mad. I got

85

over that before lunch." Minnow shrugged. "The reason I came is I found a place to go swimming. See, I brought my suit."

"Oh, good. Where?"

"I have to show you the place. It's secret."

Hollis realized she would be insulted if he smiled, so he said, "All right, wait just a minute. I'll go get my suit."

He shut the door and went in. Minnow plucked her bangs and waggled her fingers, and saw the other children run down the street and around the corner toward Twenty-third Street.

Then she remembered. She put her finger in her mouth and bit till it hurt. She'd been so busy carrying on her conversation that she'd forgotten the most important thing of all. She hadn't told Hollis not to bring Khan.

The door opened, and Hollis came out. He was stuffing his swimming trunks into his pocket, and he had Khan on the leash.

"Oh I forgot to tell you, and it's terribly important—you can't bring Khan. Dogs aren't allowed in this place. I'll wait while you—"

Hollis paid no attention to her. In fact he pushed her a little out of the way and closed the door, saying, "Sh-h-h!"

"You can't—" said Minnow.

"I have to. I just told the family I was taking Khan for a walk. If I said I was going swimming, they'd want to know where and who's the lifeguard and all about it. Besides, I bet you haven't really any place to swim, but I haven't anything else to do, so I'll come."

"Well, of all the nerve! You'll see! It's about the best swimming place you ever saw, and you'll have to stand there and just *watch,* because of Khan!"

"Nuts! I could always tie him to a street sign, the way I do when I go in the supermarket."

"Oh-h," Minnow said slowly, taking hope. "All right, then. When we get close to the place and you ought to tie him up, I'll tell you, okay?"

"Okay." Hollis smiled tolerantly. "It all sounds like a pretty mysterious plot, if you ask me."

Ever since she rang the bell and actually started talking to Hollis, Minnow had forgotten she was angry at Hollis and that this was all a plot to get even with him. She didn't really care to think about it now.

She cleared her throat and described the points of interest on the block to Hollis. "That's

Ivan's house, and that's the cave his bear lived in, and my house is next door. I live on the third floor, but I'm not allowed indoors in the daytime, hardly ever.''

Hollis looked puzzled. ''Why not?''

''Oh, my mother's too busy. She weaves rugs on an enormous loom, and when she's not doing that, she's memorizing parts in plays. She wants to be an actress, but it gets terribly boring, listening to her saying the same thing over and over. It makes me want to scream. I have to rush outdoors.''

Hollis grinned. ''I bet it isn't really as bad as that.''

''I'll tell you something else. It's a secret. I never even told Ivan.'' Minnow paused and looked up, to get Hollis's full attention. ''My mother never spanked me. Never in her whole life. Isn't that awful?''

Hollis really laughed. ''What's so bad about that?''

''Well everybody else's mother spanks them!''

''Oh. Well, how about your father? Can't you get him to?''

Minnow said gloomily, ''I hardly ever see him.

He's always working in his stupid old law office."

"I guess that's really tough then. Say, is your mother Sophia Vanderpane? She's an actress— she's in a show on Broadway that my mother saw—and I know she lives on this block."

"No, that's C.C.'s mother."

"Who's C.C.?"

"Oh, just a kid."

Hollis said, "My mother said Sophia Vanderpane had a son about my age, and she hopes I'll get to know him, and then she'll get to know *her*. She thinks actresses are wonderful."

"So do I," said Minnow. "I'm going to be an actress when I grow up."

"I should think you'd be good at that," said Hollis.

"Do you? Do you really?" Minnow skipped and twirled. She just loved walking down the avenue talking about her career with Hollis. "Do you think I could be really tragic? I want to die for hours, all over the stage."

"Well, now, I don't know. Comedy might be more your dish." Minnow scowled, and Hollis went on, "I think you have to be more experienced to be tragic. Sophia Vanderpane is in a tragedy. Mom said she cried buckets. It's called *Away the Rain*."

Minnow didn't intend to be outdone by C.C.'s mother. "Oh, pooh! There's no reason a child can't be tragic, too. This play I'm going to be in is terribly sad. I'm a little girl dying of polio."

"Oh, you're really going to be in a play yourself?"

"Of course."

"What's it called?"

"Uh—um—*After the Storm*."

Hollis grinned, cocked his head on one side, and waggled a finger at her. "Come on, Minerva, enough is enough! Vanderpane in *Away the Rain* and you in *After the Storm*? You better get someone else to write your lines."

Minnow blazed up. "What do you know about my play? That's the trouble with you. You just pick holes in everything. Pick, pick, pick! You're a big flot. Everyone on the block knows it." She strode ahead.

The words stung as Hollis remembered the kids on the block catcalling at him. "I guess they all know you're a liar, too! Besides, who cares what the crumby kids on this block think?"

"They don't think much of *you,* that's for sure!"

For once Hollis knew Minnow was telling the truth. He walked along behind her, tense and angry. Pretty soon Minnow regretted losing her temper. She wanted to go on telling Hollis about her career.

His voice tight, Hollis said, "Guess I'll go back now. I don't really want to go swimming after all. Besides, I bet it's all a fake."

Minnow turned around and looked at him pleadingly. "Come on, don't be mad. I'm not mad any more. Where we're going is just at the end of the next block. See? Where that footbridge is."

Hollis allowed himself to be led along, but he still looked sulky. He was feeling miserable and alone-against-the-world but was rather enjoying it. Someday he'd show them all. Someday they'd be sorry.

Minnow chattered on about the hydrofoil, the new kind of speedboat that carried passengers on the East River. Hollis grunted occasionally. They started up the steps to the footbridge over the East River Drive.

In the middle of the bridge, still chatting pla-

catingly to Hollis, Minnow saw Junior and C.C. duck out of sight. They looked startled and cross. Minnow stopped short in the middle of a sentence. Everything was all wrong. She was all mixed up. She'd forgotten Khan again. There he was, walking along with Hollis, his toenails clicking on the cement. But anyway, another part of her mind wailed, I only want to be friends with Hollis. I don't want to be in this plot at all. Still walking along like a sleepwalker, Minnow thought, The only thing I want in the whole wide world is to disappear.

They went down the steps to the pier, the three of them, Hollis and Minnow silent and Khan's toenails still clicking. They walked a little way toward the water, and finally Hollis said, "All right. End of joke. You can say, 'Go jump in the river,' and then we'll go home."

In a daze Minnow looked at him, hoping somehow that her eyes could tell Hollis what she couldn't, that she hadn't meant anything, not anything at all, that it was all just stories to tell for fun.

She walked along, and at the third step she got her wish. She disappeared.

8
Rescue

More things happened inside Hollis's head in the next second than had ever happened there before in one second. At the moment Minnow disappeared he had heard running footsteps behind him. He looked over his shoulder, and there were some of the Seventeenth Street bunch coming. But they seemed to be running in slow motion so that they might never reach him. Anyhow they weren't important.

In the same second he and Khan had rushed toward the point where Minnow had dropped out of sight. It was an open manhole. Khan looked down it, pricked his ears, and barked. Hollis looked down and could see nothing, but he could hear the rush of running water.

Hollis looked out, toward the river. Seagulls were screaming and gliding overhead, but they seemed to be moving in slow motion too. Hollis looked down into the water, and there she was. There was Minnow, bobbing like a rubber doll in the East River, her hair streaming in her face and her arms thrashing wildly.

Water, that was something Hollis understood. He dropped Khan's leash, kicked off his shoes, and crouched, with his toes gripping expertly on the edge of the pier. He shot out in a flat racing dive. Dimly behind him he heard the children shouting and Khan barking.

C.C. and Junior and Toby and Louise rushed up to the edge of the pier. They saw Minnow flailing the water and shouting and choking. Then they saw Hollis, cutting through the water like a powerboat. They'd never realized any kid could swim that fast. It was nothing like their style of splashy swimming.

Hollis had hit the water and known one moment of panic. Used to swimming in competition in pools, he'd never swum in water as icy as the East River in May. But his arms and legs went into their familiar action. After the first shock he was warm and swimming easily. He reached Minnow, cupped his hand under her chin, and started back for the pier.

As he approached the pier the children stopped staring and came to life.

"There's no place to get out here!" shouted C.C.

"Come on, we'll get the policeman from the park," said Toby. She and C.C. ran toward the footbridge, shouting as they ran.

"Here, my rope!" Junior yelled. He unwound it from around his waist and let it down toward the water. It wasn't long enough to reach. Louise stood like a statue, watching him. She couldn't seem to think of anything to do. She just kept thinking, I shouldn't be here—Mother will find out.

Junior slapped her on the shoulder and she came awake. "Sit on my legs!" he ordered, and he lay on the pier, hanging over the edge to dangle the rope down further. Louise sat on his legs and grabbed hold of his belt. Hollis swam in, and he could grab the rope and hold it with one hand while he held on to Minnow with the other. He couldn't climb out with her. As soon as he stopped swimming he felt again how cold the water was.

Khan looked down at Hollis and started racing up and down a short length of pier, barking and scratching furiously. His noise and the children's shouts had collected a small crowd. Two sailors of the New York City training school boat, moored at the next pier, launched their rowboat and started for the children. A policeman running over the footbridge with C.C. and Toby blew his whistle as he ran, to summon more help.

One sailor in the rowboat spotted a man on the pier taking his shoes off. The sailor yelled, "Hey, buddy, keep your shoes on! We don't want any more of you in the river. Two crazy kids in one day is enough!"

With various bored grunts to his mate the sailor nosed the boat in and reached Minnow. He hoisted her up on the pier easily, then pulled Hollis out with considerably more grunting. In the hot May sun the two stood with their teeth chattering so they couldn't say a word. Minnow looked like a reclaimed dishmop. Hollis looked angry. Khan jumped up on him feverishly, kissing him and licking off the murky drops of East River water. Hollis whispered into his furry neck, "Yes, boy! It's all right, boy! I came back." Khan calmed down and settled to licking Hollis's shivering legs.

Hollis looked up and saw a large policeman, hands on hips, glaring down at him. "All right, young feller, what's the idea? Don't you know you can't swim in the East River? You oughta be ashamed. The little girl almost drowned!"

Hollis stared at the cop, dumbfounded. He looked around the circle of children and adults, and their faces all looked unfriendly, and water was still running down his face. He snuffled and wiped his mouth on his wet shoulder.

"I *wasn't* swimming!" He meant the words to sound firm, even defiant, but his voice cracked. He might cry, right here, dripping wet, in front of a crowd of people.

The policeman considered the two shivering children and finally slapped his perspiring forehead. "Geez, we gotta get a blanket," he said and looked around for one to appear.

One did—or at least a patrol car drew up, two

more policemen jumped out, and they put coats around the children. People at the edges of the crowd began losing interest and drifted off to continue their walks. One of the new policemen, a sergeant, took off his cap and scratched his head.

"Crazy kids swimming already, in that freezing water? What's the matter with you, young feller?"

Hollis clenched his teeth and thought, I won't say anything. I just won't. I hate them all.

Louise finally spoke up. "Officer, please, they weren't swimming. Really they weren't. Minnow fell through an open manhole and Hollis jumped in after her."

The policemen were impressed by her polite manner of speaking, but they still looked suspicious.

"What minnow?"

"What manhole?"

"Over there, see"—Louise pointed—"the manhole is open. She fell through."

The three policemen paced over to the offending manhole and stared down at it, their hands on their hips. The seagulls overhead made jeering noises.

"Geez, an open manhole!" said the first cop.

"Who could of left that open?" said the second.

The third swung around and came back to the children, pointing his finger especially at Junior and C.C. "All right, now, which one of you kids was fooling around with that manhole cover? Huh? Which one of you?"

"I didn't touch it," said Junior.

"I never even *saw* it till Minnow fell in," said C.C.

"What's this minnow bit?" the cop asked, staring at all six children uneasily. Suddenly Minnow came out of her shivering trance.

She wailed, "That's me! That's where I fell in! I fell in the river, and I almost drowned, and I want to go *home*!"

The onlookers had all drifted away, and the sailors had rowed back to their boat. Khan and the six children stood on the pier with the cops, and Minnow's wailing mixed with the gulls' shrieks.

The sergeant let out a long sigh. "Let's get these kids home."

One cop took Minnow by the arm and moved her toward the prowl car, and another said to

Hollis, "Move along, kid. We'll take you home."

Hollis hunched his shoulders under the itchy overcoat. He said, "My dog. I have to take my dog home."

"We don't need to ride the dog in the prowl car," said the cop. He turned to C.C. and Junior. "Hey, you kids, you take the dog home, see?"

"He bites," said Junior.

The cop glowered at Hollis again. "How come you're keeping a dog that bites?"

"He doesn't bite," Hollis snapped.

Louise came forward and took the leash. She said, "It's all right. He knows me."

Hollis looked at her gratefully. It was the first really nice thing anyone had done. The cop glanced at C.C. and Junior out of the corner of his eye and muttered, "Chickens!" Then he motioned them to get started. The sergeant and the other cop got in the prowl car with Minnow and Hollis and started off. They moved only a few feet. The sergeant stopped and yelled to the one cop remaining on the pier.

"Hey, Mac, how about putting the cover back on the manhole?"

9

Home on the Block

The radio in the prowl car crackled out routine announcements and inquiries. The sergeant reported to his precinct that the children who had fallen in the river were safe and he was taking them home.

"Any medical report?" came the inquiry.

"Nope. They're both all right. No harm done."

"Right. Give the parents a hard time. They shouldn't let 'em play on the pier. What address you taking them to?"

The sergeant looked at Hollis, who gave his address, and the sergeant repeated it over the

103

radio and then clicked off. Minnow was still sniffling and sobbing. Hollis said, "I don't know her address, but I know which house it is."

Minnow bit her lip and stopped crying. She crossed the fingers of both hands hard, shut her eyes, and murmured, "*Make* Mommy be home! Make Mommy be home!"

When they stopped at her house, she ran in and rang the right doorbell and rushed up the stairs ahead of the police. Her mother was home. Minnow shucked off the policeman's coat and flung herself, still wet, at her mother and burst out crying again. Between sobs she howled, "I *fell*! I fell *in*!"

The policeman managed to interrupt enough to get the correct name and address, but he gave up on delivering the lecture about children playing on the pier. He felt sure Minnow's mother was going to start crying any minute too, and he backed quickly out.

The other children were already sitting on the stoop when the prowl car pulled up in front of Hollis's house. They had run all the way, and Khan was sprawled on the sidewalk, panting. He jumped up to greet Hollis.

Hollis picked up the leash and handed the policeman the coat. He was all warm now, and he hoped the police would just leave him, and maybe he could get inside and change his clothes without explaining anything to his parents.

"Thank you, sir," he said to the sergeant and started up the stoop.

"Take it easy, kid. I gotta talk to your father."

Hollis sighed and watched the policeman march up the stairs and ring the bell. He could just imagine how his father would look if he opened the door and saw the policeman there.

While they waited, a car pulled in right behind the police car. Hollis saw that it said *Daily News* on the door, and he thought, That does it. Now I'll never hear the end of this.

A photographer got out of the *News* car and joined the knot of children at the foot of the stoop. He motioned toward Hollis. "That the kid that fell in the river, huh? What's his name?"

"He didn't *fall*," said C.C. "Minnow fell through an open manhole, and he jumped in after her! He saved her life!"

"Say—" the photographer began to look

really interested. Just then Mr. Rourke opened the front door and looked at the group, and gulped. The photographer hustled up the steps to go inside with the others.

"Aw, gee, he didn't take our pictures," said Junior.

"Well, he's got to come back out," said Toby. "He certainly *ought* to take our pictures. We were *there*."

C.C. said, "This ought to be a pretty big story. Kids don't fall through manholes every day."

Louise jumped up. "I better go home. If my mother reads about me in the *Daily News,* I'll really be *finished*. I'll watch out the window. Don't tell anyone I was there, though—promise!"

They promised, and pretty soon the two policemen came out, with the photographer trailing them and jabbering angrily.

The sergeant said, "Listen, Mac, if the guy says he doesn't want his kid's picture taken, he's got a right. It's his house, see? Don't blame me. You got the kid's name. That's all I know. Anything else you gotta get from headquarters."

The two policemen jumped into their car and

drove off, and the photographer stood on the curb with his camera swinging, looking hot and mad.

Toby said sympathetically, "Those cops weren't very nice to us either." The photographer looked at her without much interest, and she went on, "If there was anything you wanted to know about Hollis and about Minnow falling through the manhole, we could tell you. We're eyewitnesses."

The photographer smiled. "Well, who is this Minnow, anyway? Maybe I can get her picture."

"Oh, you can take pictures of *any* of us," said Junior.

"Not *him*!" the newsman said, gesturing with a shoulder toward Hollis's door.

C.C. said, "Well, they're new here. You know, they're sort of rich, stuffy people, like—" He remembered he was not supposed to mention Louise, so he didn't, but continued, "Hollis isn't a bad kid, really. You oughta see him swim!"

"Zowie! Like Chris-Craft!" said Junior.

"So he saved the little girl, huh? Now this kid, this Minnow, what's her real name?"

Toby said, "Aw, she's such a dopey little kid

108

she won't even *tell* you her right name. I know where she lives, though."

"Now you're talking. Let's go!" said the photographer.

They all trooped down the street to Minnow's house, and Junior pointed to the second bell from the right. "That's the one. I know." The bell said B. C. Jenks.

They rang it, and Minnow herself opened the door at the top of the stairs.

"It's the *News,* the *Daily News,*" C.C. announced. "He wants to take your picture and ask you all about it."

"Goody!" yipped Minnow. Then she composed her manner and said stagily, "Won't you all come in?"

She was fully recovered from her dunking and dressed in her best starched sun dress. Her mother sat beside her, still looking a little nervous, as Minnow launched into her tale. She told the *News* man that she'd fallen about fifty feet, that the river had a terrific current and was carrying her out to sea, that she couldn't swim a stroke, and she was sure there were sharks around.

"Sharks, that's ridiculous!" said Toby. "Besides, you were only about twenty feet from the pier, and you do know how to swim, only you were too—"

Minnow flared out, "It was me that fell in, you know! I just guess I know what happened!"

"You make things up," said Toby. She looked on sourly as the photographer wrote down both the true and the untrue. He took pictures of them all and wrote down all their names. Minnow tried to say her real name was just Minnow, but her mother said it was Cordelia Jenks. Toby snickered, "Hello, Delia deah!"

When the photographer got to C.C., he said, "Vanderpane—say, isn't there an actress by that name? She's in something on Broadway."

"Sophia Vanderpane," said C.C. proudly. "She's my mother."

"Well, say! So you live on this block too?"

"Sure. We're at three eleven."

"I'm at three twenty-five," said Junior.

"I'm in the big building, three thirty-one," said Toby.

The photographer paid little attention to them. He said to C.C., "You and this Hollis Rourke

must be about the same age. You pal around together, huh?"

"Oh, no, I wasn't with *him*. I hardly know
him."

The photographer raised one eyebrow and
wrinkled the other. "All you kids live on this
block, and you're all way over there at Twenty-
third Street and the river, but you didn't go together?"

Minnow was glad to grab the floor again. "*I*
went with Hollis. We were walking his dog, that
big dog named Genghis Khan—he needs a lot of
exercise. The other kids are all scared of him, so
they wouldn't *dream* of coming with us."

Toby and C.C. and Junior looked at her and
their jaws dropped. Of all the two-faced exhibi-
tions! Toby finally exploded. "We are *not* scared
of him! We walked him home!"

"You were scared, though, before," Minnow
said smugly.

There was nothing the others could say really.
Toby muttered, "You just wait. We'll get *you*!"

The photographer looked at Minnow's mother
and shook his head. "I don't get it, do you? I
thought these kids were all friends."

Mrs. Jenks gave an exaggerated shrug. "Children bewilder me, dahling! Absolutely bewilder me!"

"Yes, m'am," the *News* man sighed. "Well, I'd better get on back to the office and get these pictures printed."

"Hooray! I'm going to have my picture in the paper!" sang Minnow.

"Wait'll you see your face when *we* get through with you!" Toby whispered. "You're a rat and a fink. You really are!"

For once the others agreed with her. They got out on the sidewalk, and C.C. said, "We'll never depend on *her* again! I'll bet she told Hollis the whole plot. That's how come he brought the dog."

They no longer had any particular desire to plot against Hollis. They were just sore at being fooled by Minnow. Toby said, "I'll get Louise tomorrow, and we'll have a meeting. We've got to decide what to do about *her*."

10

The News Gets Around

When the policemen brought Hollis in, Mr. and Mrs. Rourke were quite upset. First they thought he must have done something wrong, and then they realized he might have drowned. Mrs. Rourke wanted to call a doctor.

"Aw, Mom!" Hollis growled. "I just had an accidental swim. There's nothing wrong with me."

Mrs. Rourke murmured about germs and filthy water, and the sergeant cleared his throat and said, "M'am, a bunch of young children shouldn't be allowed to play over on that pier without someone in charge. It's lucky your son is such a fine swimmer and help was nearby, but—"

"I don't know anything about any *bunch* of children," Mr. Rourke objected. "Hollis simply went to take the dog for a walk."

The sergeant looked disapprovingly at Hollis. "There was a whole mess of kids with you. How about that?"

"They weren't *with* me. They just happened to *be* there."

"Huh!" the sergeant snorted. "Just happened, my foot!"

With his smooth business voice Mr. Rourke took over: "My family just moved here, officer, and I don't really think my son is acquainted with many of the neighborhood children. In any event, I'm glad no harm's been done, and I'm certainly grateful to you men for being right there on the job."

The sergeant let himself be moved toward the door.

"Don't mind if I take a picture, sir? I guess your son's quite a hero." The *Daily News* man didn't wait for any answer. He just swung his camera into position.

"I certainly do mind!" snapped Mr. Rourke. "A little accidental swim is no reason to plaster his picture all over the papers. Hollis, you can go along and change now."

"Well, he rescued the little girl who fell through—"

Mr. Rourke didn't give the *News* man any chance to argue. He started herding them all toward the door, saying, "Tch, tch, tch, some child got careless playing and tumbled in. No need to make anything of it. Good day, gentlemen."

The policemen were more than glad to get out without doing any explaining about open manholes, so when the photographer tried to pin them down about the accident, they brushed him off.

Mr. Rourke almost fell into his scrambled egg the next morning when the maid handed him a copy of the *Sunday News*. The maid pointed to a headline:

BANKER'S SCION
RESCUES MOPPET
IN OPEN MANHOLE

"Our Hollis is a hero!" the maid exclaimed. "They should of put his picture in, they should of really! Look at that. They put in pictures of all those other kids!"

"Thank goodness I got that man out of here," Mr. Rourke muttered before he started to read. He finished the first paragraph and looked at Hollis in amazement. "What's all this about the child falling through an open manhole? You never said anything about that! Did they make that up?"

"No, she did fall through," said Hollis.

"Good heavens, boy, why didn't you tell us?"

Hollis almost said that no one had asked him, but he realized that would sound rude. He shrugged. "She was just out in the river when I went after her. It didn't seem important."

"Why, it's a public disgrace! That child's parents should sue the City of New York! And imagine those officers standing here and covering up a thing like that! They didn't say one word about a manhole."

Mrs. Rourke said, "You didn't really give them a chance to say much, dear." Mr. Rourke put his head back in the newspaper.

When Mrs. Rourke got a chance to see the paper herself, she immediately spotted C.C. Vanderpane in the picture. "Why, Hollis, I *told* you Sophia Vanderpane lived on this block and had a son your age! You wretched boy, why didn't you tell me you knew him?"

"I don't know him. He just happened to be over there." His mother pushed the picture over to him. The photographer had taken it in Minnow's house, showing her talking to her friends, C.C. and Junior and Toby.

"That rotten little liar, she knew they were there all the time!" Hollis exclaimed before he thought.

"Whatever do you mean?" asked his mother.

"Uh—nothing. Well, she didn't tell me she was meeting her friends over there."

"Goodness, dear, you mustn't call her a liar just for that. And you mustn't be so standoffish about meeting other friends."

"Uh-huh."

"Don't *grunt,* Hollis! Now, when you see the Vanderpane boy and these other children again, speak up and be friendly. You certainly know them now, after a thing like this."

Hollis almost grunted again, but he remembered in time and said, "Yes, mother."

He didn't much want to go out that day. He had a feeling everyone would know he was that kid the story in the paper was about, and they would ask him questions. Khan had to go out, so finally they went, and no one on the block seemed to notice him at all. He saw C.C. and Junior in the yard by the Vanderpane's house, so he turned and walked down the block the other way. Ivan was playing in front of his house, and as soon as he saw Hollis he came toward him, holding out his hand to Khan.

"I'm not scared anymore, am I?" he said.

"Nope. You and Khan are friends."

"I read about you in the paper," said Ivan. "Why didn't they put your picture in, instead of just Minnow's?"

"Oh, Daddy didn't want them to."

"You must be awfully brave to dive into the river."

"Uh-uh. You don't have to be brave. You just have to know how to swim. I've been swimming for years."

"I don't know how to swim. I'd drown," said Ivan, his eyes round and sorrowful.

118

"It's easy. You ought to learn," said Hollis. Just then Ivan's mother called out the window to him to come in. Hollis went on around the block with Khan. He'd forgotten about C.C. and Junior, and when he came around the corner of Seventeenth Street, there they were.

Junior poked C.C. "Here he comes."

The boys knew they'd have to say something to each other now, and they were all embarrassed.

Their eyes met, and Khan stopped to sniff. "Uh—hi," said Hollis.

Junior patted Khan and said, "All the time we thought he was fierce. Really he just wants to play."

C.C. said, "What's his name? We didn't know what to call him."

"Genghis Khan."

"What?" said C.C.

"Kenkisskan?" sputtered Junior.

"Genghis Khan. You see, I thought he'd be fierce and a great watch dog and everything." Hollis saw that C.C. and Junior were still puzzled, so he explained, "Genghis Khan was the leader of the Mongols, back in the Middle Ages, and he conquered all of Siberia and Russia and killed hundreds of people, and he was really a terror.''

C.C. and Junior looked at each other and both thought the same thing: Imagine naming your dog after someone in a history book!

C.C. said, ''I guess maybe we studied about him once in school, but I don't exactly remember.''

Nobody could think of anything much more to say. Finally Hollis grunted, ''Uh—I guess I better be getting home. Got a lot of homework to do.''

''So long,'' said C.C. and Junior. They stood with their hands in their pockets, watching him go.

''No one could *have* to do their homework on Saturday morning,'' said Junior.

''Yeah. I guess he's a pretty studious type. He sure can swim, though, you gotta admit that.''

''He sure can,'' Junior agreed.

C.C. went home for lunch, and his father said, ''Hi, Famous. People recognize you out there— ask you for your autograph or anything? How'm

I going to keep up with you and your mother?
I never had my picture in the paper."

"Well, go jump in the river!" C.C. said.

"How is the boy who jumped in? Did you see
him this morning?" his mother asked.

"Yeah, I saw him. He's okay."

His mother said, "I've never seen him with
you kids. He's always just walking that dog by
himself. How come you were all over at the East
River together?"

"We weren't. I was over there with Junior
and some of the other kids, and this Rourke kid
just happened to come by, walking his dog."

C.C.'s father gave him a thoughtful look.
After a bit he said, "Did you ever ask this kid
if he'd *like* to do something with you, like skate
or play ball or whatever you're doing?"

"Um—no."

"Well, how about it? Maybe he'd like to play
ball, instead of walking the dog alone, but he
doesn't want to horn in unless someone asks
him."

"I don't think he likes to play ball much."

"Well, *ask*! That's all. He can say no. I've got
nothing against you sticking with Junior, but

sometimes you two just stick like glue and you don't give a new kid a chance."

"Okay," C.C. said. "As a matter of fact, Junior and I were just talking to him. He said the dog's name is Genghis Khan."

"That's quite a name. Is he fierce?"

"Nah, he looks it, but he's really like a kitten. I never even *heard* of this Genghis Khan character."

"You have to read books," said his father, not entirely joking.

"Umm. This Hollis kid reads a lot of books, I guess. He's that kind of a kid."

C.C.'s parents exchanged a glance, and they all went on with their lunch.

In the one room apartment in which Junior, his parents, and his married sister lived, Junior carefully cut the picture and story out of the *Sunday News* and pinned it up on the wall. His family gathered around and exclaimed with pleasure. Then Junior read the article to them, translating it into Spanish, as his parents spoke poor English. His mother said she was never going to step on another manhole cover as long as she lived. His father said he had better not let

the police catch him any place he wasn't supposed to be.

Through just one wall, but in a big modern
apartment building, lived Toby and her mother.
Toby was sitting in the big living room, feeling
unaccustomedly gloomy, almost weepy. Her
mother was banging dishes around in the
kitchen, the way she always did when she'd had
to talk to Toby's father on the phone.

Often Toby had secretly felt quite glad that
her parents were divorced. She could persuade
her mother to let her do almost anything. Also,
not having a husband to sit with in the evening,
her mother often took her to restaurants and
theaters, and when she met her father on weekends, he took her special places too.

It was a pretty good way to live, she thought,
most of the time. Except like now, when everything had popped like a soap bubble. Her father
had called up about the story in the *News,* and
he had been angry that her mother let her go
over to the East River without an adult. Now
her mother was angry too because Toby hadn't
even told her she was going to the river.

Toby pounded a sofa cushion with her fist.

The thing is, she suddenly realized, they're not either of them really angry at *me*. I'm just an excuse for them to get angry at each other. I'm just like an old bone two dogs fight over. She started really crying and went in the bathroom and locked the door.

In the DeWitt household Miranda, the nurse, showed the story in the *News* to Mrs. DeWitt. "That Hollis Rourke—the one who saved the little girl—he's the boy Louise goes to dancing school with, isn't he?"

Mrs. DeWitt nodded, and Louise watched cautiously, pretending not to know anything about the story. Mrs. DeWitt noticed Toby and C.C. in the picture and passed the paper on to Louise. She said, "I'm certainly glad *you're* not roaming the streets like that. Imagine those children's parents letting them go play on a pier by themselves!"

Miranda sniffed disapprovingly too. "It's lucky that Rourke boy is such a good swimmer, or the little girl would have drowned."

Mrs. DeWitt continued, "Children shouldn't be left alone to pick up their own friends on the street anyway. When you meet children at school or dancing school, I know they'll be the right sort of people. I suppose Hollis was just walking his dog over by the river. He wasn't with this gang of children at all, was he?"

"Oh, no, I'm sure he wasn't *with* them," said Louise, very glad to be able to be quite truthful for once.

When Ivan's mother called him to come in, he found that Minnow and her parents were there, having a late Sunday breakfast. Minnow's father had just been to the Rourkes' house to thank Hollis officially for saving Minnow. He felt embarrassed that she'd been there at all.

Ivan's mother said to Minnow's mother, "Dolly, I just have to say this: I've always *known* something would happen to Minnow, the way you let her run around anywhere, and I'm only glad she's safe this time, and I hope you'll keep a closer rein on her. Of course it wasn't your fault that manhole cover was off. That's scandalous, absolutely scandalous! You should sue the city."

"I would," said Mr. Jenks, Minnow's father,

"except the little minx isn't hurt a bit."

"What did happen, exactly, Minnow?" asked Mr. Hedge, Ivan's father.

Minnow launched into her tale, which got better every time she told it. When she told how she was out in the river, screaming for help, Mr. Hedge said to Mr. Jenks, "Doesn't she know how to swim?"

"Yes, she swims pretty well," Mrs. Jenks said. "Minnow, why didn't you swim instead of screaming?"

"Well—um, it was cold, and there were all these seagulls—that's it, there were all these seagulls zooming around me, beating their wings in my face and. . . ."

Mr. Jenks looked disgustedly at his wife and said, "Can't you teach that child *ever* to tell the truth?"

Ivan's father interrupted judiciously, "Most of these children think they can swim better than they can. Now, Ivan here can swim, but—"

"I can't swim," Ivan contradicted him.

"I taught you myself, last summer. You took several strokes. Besides"—Mr. Hedge looked at his wife—"you've been taking him to the pool for lessons, haven't you?"

"Well, we don't go quite as often as I'd planned. You see, it's my sitter day for the baby, and I like to get my hair done, and Ivan doesn't like to go in the water without me, and—"

"And, and, and! You girls just never do what you say you're going to do about these kids." Mr. Hedge looked to Mr. Jenks for support.

"I'll say they don't," said Mr. Jenks. "Just put off and put off."

"Well!" Mrs. Jenks bristled. "You never do *anything* with Minnow, not anything! You just run off to that office every time I suggest a single thing!"

"I have to work," said Mr. Jenks.

Mr. Hedge put the fingertips of his two hands together thoughtfully over his well-fed stomach. "Well, now, perhaps it isn't the girls' fault either. We all get distracted from things we mean to do, and it also occurs to me that there are some things children learn better from others than from—ah—their parents. Like swimming. Now this boy who rescued Minnow seems to be some kind of champion swimmer. Couldn't we hire him as a sort of swimming-sitter and teacher to take the children to the pool?"

"What a marvelous idea!" exclaimed his wife.

Minnow's father grumbled, "She doesn't need any expensive lessons. She just needs a good whack on the fanny!"

"Darling," began Mrs. Jenks, "your ideas of child psychology are just *so* old-fashioned—"

Minnow interrupted, "Daddy, why don't *you* take me swimming, and we won't have to have any arguments or expensive lessons, and I'll do just what you tell me. Okay, Daddy?"

"Uh-oh," said Mr. Jenks. "I've been had."

Mr. Hedge went to call on the Rourkes. "You must be very proud of your son," he said to the parents. "It was just splendid the way he rescued that little girl."

"Hollis is such an experienced swimmer, I guess it just came naturally," said Mr. Rourke.

"He's won several prizes at camp," added Mrs. Rourke, and Hollis wished she wouldn't bring *that* up.

"Well, I didn't butt in here just to offer congratulations," said Mr. Hedge. "I—uh—I have a problem. I think it's very important for every child to know how to swim, for his own safety, and my little boy, Ivan, seems to be—well, afraid. I've taught him to swim a little, but. . . ."

Mr. Hedge seemed to be floundering, himself, so Hollis said, "Oh, I know Ivan. He's sort of afraid of everything. But he gets over it. He used to be afraid of Khan, but now he loves him."

"You know my Ivan already—that's wonderful! Then I'm sure you could help him. You see, I'd like to hire you to take him to the pool once a week and work with him. I'd pay you just as we do our baby-sitter, only you'd be a—a swim-sitter." Mr. Hedge beamed.

"Oh, sure, that'd be fine. I need something to do on Saturdays anyway, and I like Ivan."

Hollis's parents beamed too because for once he was speaking up and acting enthusiastic about something. They settled that Hollis would start with Ivan the next Saturday.

11
End of the Flot

The next Saturday Minnow and Ivan were playing outside his house. Minnow's father had promised to take her swimming, but he hadn't waked up yet. Ivan was waiting excitedly for Hollis to come, and he wouldn't concentrate properly on anything else.

Finally he jumped up and pointed down the block. "Here he comes!"

Minnow felt a frightened tingling in the bottom of her stomach. She couldn't think what she should say to Hollis, exactly, and she wondered what he would say to her.

He said nothing, absolutely nothing, to her. "Hi, Ivan. You all ready? Let's go." And they went.

Ivan ranged himself beside Hollis proudly. Over his shoulder he said to Minnow, "See you later, maybe."

Minnow watched them go and clenched her fists so hard they hurt. Hollis hated her, C.C. and Junior and Toby hadn't spoken to her all week, and her father wouldn't wake up. She had to loosen up her clenched fists, so she threw her hands in the air and jumped up and down and shouted, "I hate everyone! I'm going to run away!"

A lady passing by smiled and said, "Now, now, dear, better run home and find mother." That made Minnow angrier still. She darted across Seventeenth Street and around the corner of First Avenue. She looked back and saw Hollis and Ivan talking together and the strange lady looking rather worried. She decided she would join the gang of tough kids on Sixteenth Street.

"Now, about Minnow. We've got to decide." Toby stood on the stoop and addressed the meeting, which was assembled in C.C.'s little yard and consisted of C.C. and Junior and Louise.

"I respectfully submit," went on Toby, "that this person behaved like a sneak and a rat. She knew Khan wasn't fierce, but she didn't tell us. That's one. She didn't tell Hollis not to bring Khan to the East River. That's two. She may have fallen in the river on purpose so he could rescue her. That's—"

"That's stupid. We all saw her fall through the manhole," said C.C., who disliked Toby when she got in one of these presiding-over-formal-meeting moods. He liked Minnow around at meetings, to break them up.

Louise said, "She couldn't have fallen in on purpose. And maybe she couldn't stop him bringing the dog."

Toby considered. "All right, it was an accident. But we still know she's a rat, and she's not a loyal member of the gang."

"I think she *likes* Hollis anyway," said Junior.

"That's right!" Toby shouted. "See—she didn't even *want* to get Hollis. She just pretended. She was a traitor from the start."

"So what? None of us want to get Hollis anymore. Maybe he reads too many books, but he's not bad really," C.C. said.

"That's beside the point," Toby jumped up. "We *did* want to get him *then,* and she pretended to. Why, she practically made up the whole plot!"

Louise and Junior nodded, and Toby, seeing that she had a majority, said, "I move we vote. All in favor of expelling Minnow from the club mark a black X on your paper."

She collected the ballots and said, "Motion passed, by three votes. Somebody didn't mark their ballot."

C.C. said. "I didn't, because I'm not in favor. There's no point in voting if we all agree. Besides, I think expelling her is stupid. What difference does it make?"

"You mean you're still going to play with her?" said Toby.

"I might. If I felt like it."

Toby said, "Maybe there are some other people who shouldn't be in this gang, if they're not going to abide by the gang's decisions."

"Oh, go abide by yourself!" C.C. exchanged

glances with Junior and added, "Or expel me. Go ahead."

Seeing the two-to-two line up, Toby cleared her throat and said, "Let's quit wasting time. We ought to plan the next campaign."

"Against who?" said Junior.

"Well, let's get the Sixteenth Street gang," said Toby. "They're our real enemies. They bombed our fort."

"Think I'll roller skate," said C.C.

"Me too," said Junior. "Let's get our hockey sticks."

Toby sniffed. "All right, I know you're just chicken! So go ahead and roller skate. Me and Louise will spy out the terrain."

The two girls sidled off to the park, and C.C. and Junior went to get their skates. The meeting hadn't amounted to much.

When Minnow walked around the corner of Sixteenth Street, there were two or three big boys and a girl in very tight pants in front of the candy store. Led by the girl, they walked toward her, shuffling their feet, keeping their arms at their sides, and snapping their fingers.

Minnow smacked her hand to her forehead, said, "Oh my goodness, I forgot!" and turned and ran. The kids behind her whistled rudely.

Minnow went up to her apartment, and her mother said, "Daddy's still asleep. He was working very late last night. I don't think you'd better count on swimming."

"He has to! He promised!" Minnow cried.

"Well, you know how daddys are. They have other things to worry about."

"So do I! All my friends are perfectly horrible, and Daddy *promised*! He has to come!" Minnow saw her father's big shoes on the floor and picked them up and hurled them—one, two, bang, bang—against his door.

"Minnow!" shouted her mother.

Her father opened the bedroom door and came out like an unhibernated bear. He roared, "Stop that racket!"

"I won't! I hate everybody! You promised!" yelled Minnow.

Her father took one great step across the room, picked her up, delivered one great spank to her blue-jeaned bottom, and put her down. Then he stalked into the bathroom and slammed the door and turned on the shower.

"Wah-h-h-h!" yowled Minnow.

"Oh, Benjamin!" gasped her mother. Then she hurried into the kitchen and fussed about getting breakfast.

Minnow curled up in the big armchair and cried as hard as she could. After a while she heard the shower turn off, and her father went into the kitchen, and she heard the clink of dishes and ordinary conversation. She stopped crying and tried to hear what they were saying, but couldn't. She started a new burst of crying, but it didn't go well. She rolled on her back and put her legs over the arm of the chair and let her head dangle down. She thought, I really don't feel much like crying anymore. I feel quite good, and I still want to go swimming, but now maybe Daddy won't. She thought hard and remembered that she had two dimes left from her lemonade money. She ran and got them and strolled into the kitchen, clinking them in her hand.

"Look, Daddy, I earned money selling lemonade, and I saved up two dimes, so we could have Cokes after swimming. You and me."

Mr. Jenks winked at his wife, then he said, "All right, let's go."

That afternoon Minnow was sitting by herself on the stoop, and she thought, The trouble with swimming is it doesn't take long enough. Down the block she could see the other kids gathered in C.C.'s yard. Ivan was with them. Minnow frowned. She had almost never been left out of the bunch before, and she didn't like it.

Just because I forgot to tell Hollis not to bring the dog—they don't have to get so mad about a little thing like that. Anyone could forget. She knew that wasn't really what made them mad, but she tried to convince herself.

She pulled a stub of chalk out of her pocket and drew pictures of all the children. Then she drew an enormous dog to eat them all up. Then she sighed and looked around.

Hollis came out of his house with Khan and crossed the street. Minnow jumped up and followed, as soon as he was out of sight, into the park. She tracked them carefully, always running silently on the grass and hiding behind good fat trees and bushes. Neither Hollis nor Khan ever looked around. Getting a little bored, Minnow closed in, moving less carefully and not really hiding at all.

Hollis walked as he always did, head thrust down, looking at his own feet. Khan heard Minnow. He looked around, pulled at his leash, and finally sat down firmly and gave his short, happy, let's-play bark.

Hollis looked around irritably, and Minnow ducked behind a very skinny tree, from which she stuck out on both sides.

"You're not fooling anyone," he said.

"I know," said Minnow, sauntering out and cocking her head to look up at the leaves and clouds.

"So, quit following me."

"Oh, I'm not following you personally. It's an experiment." Minnow pulled her eyes down from the clouds, frowned busily, and made three marks on the back of her hand with the chalk. "You see, I can track an ordinary adult around this park for nineteen minutes without their knowing. Ordinary child, eleven minutes. Child with dog, only three minutes, twenty seconds. This indicates that—"

"You're nuts, that's what. Don't you *ever* stop making things up?"

"It gets dull if I don't. I'll race you to that big

bush with the red flowers!'' Minnow didn't want to give Hollis time to ask her too many questions. She shot off, and Khan leaped after her, so Hollis had to run too. He found it felt good to be running. The wind fanned through his hair, and he enjoyed the startled expressions on the faces of bench-sitters as he tore past them.

Minnow reached the bush and crawled deep into its shady interior. Hollis and Khan plumped down beside her, and they were all busy panting and cooling off for a bit. Minnow broke off a twig and started marking a picture in the packed dirt.

Hollis watched her a while and said, ''Listen. Maybe it doesn't matter if you make up spy experiments, or parts in plays, or living in New Hampshire. But it sure matters if you make up a swimming expedition to get me over on a pier for some kids to jump on me. You know what that makes you?''

Minnow bent close over her dirt drawing and shook her head.

''A rat. Just a rat.''

Khan panted noisily in the silence under the bush. Hollis reached over and pushed Minnow's forehead up, so that she had to look at him. He said, "See?"

Minnow looked at him through a teary blur, and she knew there was only one thing she could say. "I'm sorry."

She looked so sad that Hollis had to smile. "Well, it's all right. Nothing bad happened."

"I didn't want anything to happen. I just sort of forgot which part I was playing."

"That's what I mean. You can't play parts *all* the time. Sometimes you have to be y—"

"Ouch!" Hollis yelped and sat up as someone banged his ankles with a walking stick. His feet had been sticking out from under the bush. A man parted the branches, stuck his pink shiny face through, and glared at them.

"Don't be hiding under the bushes with the little girl! Come on, get out here with the other kids!" he said.

"We're not hiding. We're just sitting where it's cool," said Hollis.

"I know you're up to something! Come on out," said the man.

Minnow bounced out from under the bush and stamped her foot. "I know what you're up to, I

do! You just better leave us alone and go make your annual contribution to the Flot Foundation! Hurry up, before they kick you out!"

The man's jaw dropped with astonishment, and he backed away a little. Minnow continued to glare at him, and he moved away, twitching his shoulders and humphing to himself. From a distance he shook his cane at them and then went off.

"How are we *ever* going to get rid of them?" Minnow asked Hollis.

"Who?"

"These flots. They're all over."

"What is all this flot business?" Hollis asked, looking a little suspicious again.

"Oh, it all started in the park one day when a lot of these grown-ups kept trying to boss us around, always trying to mind *our* business. Then we came home, and you and Khan chased us off when we wanted to watch the men moving the piano. So we called you a flot too. But you're not one, really."

"Ummmm," Hollis said. "I guess I was, sort of."

"Well anyway, it doesn't matter now, because

you're not. But we've got to get rid of them."

Minnow pulled her skip-rope out of her pocket and skipped with fierce concentration, until two ladies on a park bench said in unison, "Little girl, don't skip here! You'll wake the babies."

"*My* baby," said Minnow, looking them right in the eye, "just loves me to skip. He sits up and *begs* me to skip!"

"Go on, little girl. Find your mother."

"I can't. She's in the hospital. She's terribly—" Hollis choked laughing and pulled her away. They started home.

"You see," said Minnow, as they crossed Seventeenth Street and out of the corner of her eye she saw the other children still in C.C.'s yard, "*they* stick together. They flot together. But *we* get all mixed up fighting among ourselves."

"Umm," said Hollis.

In C.C.'s yard the children were in a circle, throwing pennies at a chalked spot because no one could think of anything better to do.

"Psst! Minnow's coming! Don't anyone notice her!" Toby ordered. C.C. straightened up and gazed impersonally at the rooftops.

146

Minnow looked scornfully at their backs. Stupids, who do they think they're fooling, she thought. Then she leaped up the stoop, flapped her arms like a rooster and crowed:

"Hear ye! Hear ye! Hear ye! The war with the flots is hear ye reopened! Hollis and Genghis Khan are now on our side!"

"Who said?" Toby growled.

"I said. There's no time to lose. A big shiny-faced flot tried to break Hollis's ankle with his cane, and another female one tried to stop me skipping rope."

The others looked at Hollis with interest. "Did a guy really hit you? With his cane?"

Hollis explained what happened, and Toby said, "If he really hit you, you could sue."

"Pooh!" said Minnow. "We don't sue! We retaliate!"

"Well, we can do a lot more with Khan on our side," said Toby. "Besides, seven is a better number for a club. You can vote better. All right, what's the plan?"

"Lou-*ise*!" Miranda's voice called, and Louise looked up at the church clock and sighed.

"Five o'clock. I guess I've got to go."

"I'll walk along with you," said Hollis, and Louise was glad she didn't have to pretend to hate him anymore.

Minnow watched the two of them with a slight frown and tapped her foot. In her school teacher voice, she said, "Come along, Ivan, your mother will be looking for you." They walked along behind the other two.

As Louise was saying good night to Hollis, Minnow jumped up on the stoop. She raised her arm at the elbow and pointed her index finger at Louise and Hollis:

"Remember now! Flot fighters of the world—unite!"

HARPER TROPHY BOOKS
you will enjoy reading

HARPER & ROW, PUBLISHERS, INC.
10 East 53rd Street, New York, N.Y. 10022